Return to Redemption Ridge

First Edition, June 2012

ISBN: 978-0-9856887-0-7

For information visit:
www.BELCHERBOOKS.com

Cover Design by George Belcher
Book design by Maureen Cutajar

Return to Redemption Ridge

A Novel by
George Eugene Belcher

Dedication

To my soul mate, Carole, and my loving daughters,
Tracy and Beth.

Acknowledgements

As an adult, I joined contemporaries, parents, and grandparents in prayer while loved ones continued to fight for our freedom abroad.

As a child, I sat in awe of the stories told by wise men and women who were born in 1900 or earlier. My parents, grandparents, and many of my neighbors and extended family were among these strong individuals. Some were veterans who served in two world wars. Some were "Gold Star Mothers" who lost children in the fight for America's freedom. Their stories told of good years and bad, how each dealt with adversity, sadness, joy, and opportunity. They inspired *Return to Redemption Ridge*.

The character of Zack in the book is fictitious and his personality a fusion of many. However, when this character speaks, I hear the voice of a dear family friend whom in my youth I called "uncle". Uncle Pete's daughter, and my treasured friend, Claudette LaBonte, added her clear-eyed proofreading to the final text.

I wrote the original manuscript in the first-person narrative, from the "I" point of view, while Mary, my dear mother was living her ninetieth year. The year was 1990. In 2011, after dusting off the unpublished manuscript, I rewrote it in the third person narrative, from the "observer" point of view.

My heartfelt appreciation goes out to the angels who assisted me with test reading and proofreading this manuscript before publication. Among them, my bright cousin, Joan Gentile, my dear and perspicacious friend, Ruth Ehrenberg, and new friend and trained reading-teacher, Barbara Lentini.

Maureen Cutajar, my professional consultant/book designer, among other things, taught me that multiple quote signs at the end of a sentence are okay with the *Chicago Manual of Style* when applicable.

A special thank you to the most patient person I have ever known, Carole, my loving wife and best friend for over half a century. Carole lived the book with me.

Responsibility for final proofing, and any errors of omission or commission are mine to bear.

Prologue

The Appalachian Mountain range becomes "The Berkshires" as it passes through Western Massachusetts on its northern journey. The Mohican Native American tribe roamed the region until the early eighteenth century when the first English settlers and frontiersmen appeared, constructing farms and homesteads. In the Gilded Age of the nineteenth century, the country's elite built summer retreats throughout the popular New England hills. In the early twentieth century, World War I, the Great Depression, and the introduction of the income tax led to economic decline, ending the Gilded Age. Many of these structures fell to neglect.

One farm still stands, its plateau meadows sprawling from the cliff base of Redemption Ridge. Here, at the base of the foreboding outcropping, a 1990 pre-Christmas blizzard traps a young journalist.

Centuries of tragic accidents, suicides, and murders feed stories that Redemption Ridge holds magical power. Many people claim to have seen apparitions around the ridge and the farm, fueling the belief that spirits haunt the area in quest of justice or salvation.

The purpose of Jonathan Dunquin's visit is to interview the reclusive billionaire Zackarie Todd. To his surprise, Jonathan finds the ninety-year-old alone at the two hundred-year-old farm. His only companions an aging retriever, two cats, and five prize horses. From the moment of his arrival, Jonathan is plagued with visions. At times, he wants to bolt and return to New York. He discovers that a woman, whom he never met, influenced his life for years. And, that same woman had arranged his visit. Years after her death, she continues to control his destiny.

When Jonathan accepted the surprise invitation, he did not expect to be dealing with the paranormal or the possibility of re-incarnation.

Is it possible that Jonathan lived before in the shadow of Redemption Ridge?

Despite frequent urges to flee, Jonathan stays—held by an unseen force.

Chapter One

April 1806

Horses' hoofs scramble for footing, Emmett leaps to his feet in the carriage. He throws his full weight back, straining at the reins. Two thousand pounds of falling animals yank Emmett from Hope's panicked grasp. Her scream of terror echoes from the cliff wall—the last sound of his beloved's voice rings in Emmett's ears—then, black silence.

Consciousness returns slowly, Emmett cannot move, he tastes mud. Rain floods his eyes, blurring his vision. His broken body shakes violently. Each gasp for breath produces searing pain. He prays that somehow Hope has survived.

"Hope!" He screams, "Dear God let her be alive—Hope!" The storm drowns out Emmett's anguished cries.

Six months earlier, Emmett Morgan and Hope McBride planned their life together.

Indian summer brought mild, October weather to the Massachusetts Berkshires. It was the last day that the betrothed couple would sit in the lilac-laden gazebo before Hope returned to Boston to spend the winter.

The lattice pavilion provided a place of shade, Emmett's first gift to his bride-to-be. Together they surrounded the structure with a flower garden alive with color. Emmett also had made the bench on which they sat.

Hope's head rested on Emmett's shoulder. She twists the stem of a chrysanthemum between her fingers and peers up at him with sky-blue eyes. Coquettishly she tickles his square jaw with the last bloom of the season. Emmett's eyes mirror her love. Hope's expression darkens. She looks away to hide tears.

"Emmett, I'm going to miss you so. This is my home now. I wish I could stay and never leave you."

Emmett felt the need to swallow before he spoke, fearing his words would catch in his throat, "It would be the answer to my prayers if you stayed."

"Perhaps I can purchase furniture and curtains in Boston," Hope forces herself to brighten. "It would help the time pass," she bolts upright, turns, and breaks into a wide smile, "I can buy a cradle. We can decorate the nursery when I return."

In his forceful manner, Emmett replied, "No, that is my job. I will build my first child's cradle with my own hands while you are away."

Hope McBride was the only woman to melt the quarry owner's heart; however, even she could not bend the masterful Emmett Morgan's will.

Emmett met the woman he called his fair-haired beauty while Hope visited her brother, Margate. Margate held the position of manager at the Morgan Quarry with the distinction of also being Emmett's closest friend. Hope lived and taught school in Boston. After meeting Emmett, her heart leaped to the Berkshires. It was love at first sight for both. They announced their engagement a week after meeting.

When Emmett proposed to Hope, he lived in a run-down house at the quarry.

"It is not a fit place for my wife or children," Emmett announced to Margate when he asked Hope's brother for his sister's hand in marriage, "I will build a house for my new bride."

Emmett found a scenic two hundred acres of fertile meadows, the perfect setting for the fine house he would build for his precious Hope. The land lay at the base of Redemption Ridge, the supernatural folklore of the location having no importance to the stalwart Emmett.

The summer of 1805 delivered glorious days, and construction of the new farm moved ahead quickly. Hope stayed with her brother and his family to be near the man she loved. She visited often. While Emmett supervised and labored, Hope planted flower gardens.

At the end of each workday, the gazebo was where she and Emmett shared their dreams of the future. They planned to exchange marriage vows under the fragrant trellis.

The happy couple enjoyed many leisure hours together through the blazing color of the New England autumn while the house was finished. The house was the final gem set in a perfect setting. They spent their favorite time of day watching the sunset across the valley below while basking in its glow reflected from the craggy face of the high ridge overhead.

Before the first snow of winter, Hope traveled to Boston to have her wedding dress made and prepare for her future. The gray winter dragged agonizingly slowly for both Emmett and Hope. Each wrote letters daily, proclaiming their love.

On the day of her departure, Emmett wrote Hope.

Dearest Hope,

The sun was bright this morning as we said good-bye. For me the day turned as dark as a clouded midnight. Knowing that it will be months before I hold your delicate hand again cuts deeply into my heart.

I watched the sun go down from our favorite place. In the early dusk, the face of the ridge looked as sorrowful as mine must be.

Breezes will carry your fragrance, the bright sky will remind me of your eyes, and songbirds will bring your sweet voice to me.

Day's end will hold no color without you to share our precious sunsets.

My love for you is overwhelming. I await your letters to hear your words in my heart and to rest my cheek on the paper that you put your hand to.

I am your faithful intended husband,
Emmett

The April day that Hope returned from Boston was cold, the Western Massachusetts sky blackened with storm clouds. Emmett washed, put on his best shirt, and excitedly prepared to meet Hope at the stage stop in West Stockbridge. Before leaving the house, he visited the bedroom that would be the nursery. He smiled as he gently rocked the empty cradle he lovingly made for his first-born. He ran his calloused hands over the smooth wood and allowed his mind to drift. Emmett wondered how many of his children might one day doze in this cradle.

Emmett selected the high-riding, open carriage over the low-slung, quarry wagon. Pulled by two horses, it was the best choice for fording spring-swollen streams and traveling over rutted mountain roads. He hummed to himself happily in anticipation of Hope's return. Emmett hitched his favorite horses as a show of his beloved's importance.

The stage stop reunion was as joyful as a Christmas morning. Hope leaped from the coach into Emmett's arms. Each felt the other's heart pounding as they embraced. Despite six days of punishing travel, the uncomplaining Hope beamed with joy, a testimony to the inner strength hidden by her graceful beauty.

Distant thunder and light rain did not dampen the happy couple's spirits. As they neared Redemption Ridge, they laughed when bumps jostled their frequent kisses.

Halfway up the road crossing the ridge, the storm's full fury struck, rain sheeted nearly blinding Emmett as it poured from the rim of his hat. Hope cowered against him, shivering from fear.

Emmett was glad that he and Margate agreed Hope should return to the farm that night. It was closer than Margate's house at the quarry. Emmett's live-in widowed sister was a suitable chaperone for the engaged couple.

Hope knew that the road ran perilously close to the cliff edge. She cried, "Emmett, I'm afraid. Please stop. Wait until you can see where you are going."

Emmett ignored her pleas, he trusted his horses, the warmth of their new home waited, he confidently pushed on.

Ahead, the deluge chewed a wide gash at the road's crest. Rushing water streamed over the precipice. The horses tossed their heads against the stinging torrent as they approached the unseen danger. Emmett wrapped the reins around his wrists for better control. The streaming water caught the team and they plunged into the cascade. The force snatched Emmett from Hope's grasp, pulling him into the abyss.

Hope screamed, "God help me." Moments later, she lay in the crushed wreck one-hundred feet below.

At the farmhouse, Sarah prepared a welcome supper. Over the roar of the storm, she was certain she heard screams. She grabbed a hooded cape. She dashed from the house. Guided by an unseen hand, she ran to the base of the ridge.

The storms flashing illuminated the horror. The silent bodies of Hope and the horses lay in the tangled carnage. Hope's eyes stared at the heavens, fixed in death, her hair splayed, like a golden halo.

Over the battering of the deluge, Emmett could hear Sarah's mournful cries of discovery. He knew that Hope had not survived. An ethereal glow pulsed across the heavens as Emmett waited impatiently for death to relieve his suffering

Margate blamed Emmett for Hope's death. He closed his house and took his family and all their possessions with him when he brought his sister's body back to Boston. He never returned.

Emmett survived, crippled, and destined to live a life of guilt and desolation. He closed the quarry.

Emmett wanted to join Hope and frequently pleaded with Sarah to take him to the top of the ridge cliff in his wheel chair and leave him.

Sarah became Emmett's constant companion and caregiver. She ran the farm and did all she could to comfort her brother. Spring through fall, she kept the flower gardens and the gazebo trellises blossoming. During the winter, she filled the house with dried flowers in an attempt to cheer Emmett. A deeply spiritual woman, she prayed intensely for Emmett to forgive himself. She believed in the immortality of the human soul and prayed the spirits of Emmett and Hope would have another chance to share their love.

Nothing kept the brother and sister from their daily vigil. Sarah pushed Emmett in his wheelchair up the specially built ramp into the gazebo. They watched the setting sun's reflection from the ridge until it darkened. Some evenings, the wall glowed golden, at other times, crimson. In early evening, the rock face glowered in the gloom.

Seeking reminders of Hope's tragic death became Emmett's self-imposed penance. He would stare at the ridge in storms, and watch lightning bounce angrily from the craggy surface.

When Emmett died, he bequeathed the farm to Sarah. She lived there for years and ran it as a dairy farm. Duty bound, Sarah maintained the sunset observance. One winter morning, a farm hand found Sarah in the gazebo, kneeling in prayer, frozen to death.

Before Sarah's heirs took over, the farm sat empty and forsaken. The tragic story of Hope, Emmett, and Sarah attracted lovers and curiosity-seekers there. At twilight, many observers claim to have seen apparitions of Sarah pushing Emmett in his wheelchair up the gazebo ramp.

Chapter Two

June 1842

The first sliver of sunrise lay hidden behind Redemption Ridge. In the shadowed farmhouse below, two lovers parted. Joseph buttoned his shirt over a powerful chest as he crept down the staircase, his departure softened by thick socks. He sat on the third step from the bottom and tugged on scuffed boots. He cast an expectant look at the balcony above and the naked woman who peered down at him. His heart leaped at the sight of her alabaster skin glowing in the dim morning light.

The lovers exchanged smiles and thrown kisses before Joseph slipped quietly out the door.

Rebecca Wakefield turned slowly, twisting a strand of tawny tresses around a graceful finger. She moved languidly back to the master bedroom and lingered before the full-length, mahogany-trimmed mirror, her head tilted appreciatively. One fingertip traced the fullness of her breasts. She turned to the arrangement of fresh flowers on her dressing table, and inhaled Joseph's statement of love with closed eyes. The fragrance brought back memories of forbidden kisses shared with her lover in the vine-draped gazebo. How Rebecca loved the beautiful gardens that Joseph maintained for her.

Joseph presented the freshly picked bouquet to Rebecca when he arrived after dark, the prior evening. The lovers went immediately to the attic and spent hours, as they often did, reading the love notes and journals stored in the wooden chest. The passionate expression of star-crossed lovers touched Rebecca deeply.

To Rebecca, the love letters represented a romantic treasure. To Oakwood, they were an annoyance. He sternly commanded Rebecca, that if she opened the chest, she must treat the contents with care. As a condition of the sale of the farm, he had grudgingly posted a significant bond, guaranteeing no harm would come to the chest or its contents.

The heat of passion still burned in Rebecca as she returned to bed. With Joseph, she finally knew true love. Later, Oakwood would be here, and she would again be his captive, until another business trip allowed her to continue her infidelity.

Rebecca Palmer-Wince and Oakwood Wakefield first met at one of Albany's elite social galas. Oakwood was impressively handsome and notably wealthy. Rebecca immediately saw the middle-aged bachelor's amorous interest and realized the opportunity it presented. She enjoyed teasing men and had bedded many during her twenty-eight years, but none offered what Oakwood offered—money, security, and position.

At forty-eight, Oakwood enjoyed his freedom. He knew that many of his numerous love conquests expected to trap him into marriage. The sly and maneuvering Oakwood used his fine-tuned persuasive skills on women the same way he did with the men in his business dealings, successfully, and always to his benefit.

Oakwood wanted to breed an heir before he turned fifty. He sought a suitable wife to satisfy his needs and give him a child.

Then, Rebecca Palmer-Wince appeared in his life.

The hostess that fateful evening, Madeline Kerr-Carney fancied herself a matchmaker. She was the trophy wife of the retired governor. She also enjoyed an adulterous affair with the handsome and viral Oakwood.

Madeline introduced the two with a flourish. She led Rebecca by the hand to the handsome bachelor, "Oakwood, this is my dear friend, Miss Rebecca Palmer-Wince. Rebecca, this is Oakwood Wakefield."

Madeline's face took on a cagey expression and she jokingly said, "Be careful my dear, Oakwood is incorrigible."

Oakwood bowed graciously, his dark eyes performing a surreptitious examination. He straightened to face Rebecca. She was breathtaking, porcelain features in a gilded frame. Oakwood's eyebrows rose at the sight of the astonishingly beautiful woman. Rebecca's indigo eyes met Oakwood's appreciative stare, "Good evening, Mr. Wakefield, how nice to meet you."

"Miss Wince."

Mentally, Oakwood appraised Rebecca. No gushing, no flirtatious fluttering, here was a self-assured woman. She will make the chase exciting.

Rebecca was experienced in the art of tantalizing a man. She thrilled at Oakwood's reaction to their meeting. Through the evening, the young men swarmed around the vivacious beauty. Oakwood stood apart, observing from a distance. His attention excited Rebecca.

The day following their meeting, a messenger appeared at Rebecca's door. He handed her a note and a single, rare, lavender rose. The lavender rose carries the meaning, "love at first sight."

At first, Rebecca's heart skipped with anticipation; however, the accompanying note read more like a summons than an amorous message.

Mr. Oakwood Wakefield requests the company of Miss Rebecca Palmer-Wince as his dinner guest this evening. Dinner will be served in Mr. Wakefield's residence hotel suite promptly at 7:00 PM. Mr. Wakefield's carriage will arrive at your doorstep at 6:45 PM.

Oakwood's curt note infuriated Rebecca. The nerve of the man, commanding *her,* where is the polished Wakefield charm?

Rebecca scrawled a response on Oakwood's original note. She paid the messenger generously and instructed him to procure a single, striped carnation, then, deliver it with her response to Oakwood.

The stage was set. Rebecca was proud of herself. She will teach the brazen man a lesson and push the rich bachelor to his knees. The game filled Rebecca with excited anticipation.

Upon seeing the single striped carnation in the messenger's hand, Oakwood flushed with anger, striking the flower and the written reply to the floor. He did not need to read Rebecca's notation, he knew its content.

I will not comply.

Oakwood fumed. He was unaccustomed to rejection and did not pursue Rebecca further. His anger boiled.

Rebecca did not hear from Oakwood again, she knew she overplayed her hand. Her ungracious refusal unleashed Oakwood's scorn. However, the circumstances did not deter Rebecca. Seducing Oakwood posed an invigorating challenge. She delighted in plotting her next approach.

Weeks after their meeting, Rebecca and Oakwood met again, this time, during a Sunday promenade in Washington Park. Each was with friends. All knew one another and the event was cordial and lighthearted.

Rebecca greeted Oakwood with only the slightest hint of flirtation. "Good afternoon Mr. Wakefield. How good it is to see you again. You are looking so well."

Oakwood stiffened and stated, "Indeed, Miss Wince, the pleasure is mine."

The event had been well planned; Rebecca subtly displayed many of her feminine charms. She watched as Oakwood softened to her. The hook was set.

That evening, Rebecca boldly entered the lobby of Oakwood's hotel and had her visit announced.

A bellman escorted Rebecca to Oakwood's rooms. When Oakwood opened the door, the nervous bellman retreated in haste. Without saying a word, the two pressed their bodies together in a passionate frenzy, each feeling it was they who had prevailed.

Their courtship was brief; the couple married and honeymooned in Montreal. Oakwood insisted his business interests required his return.

Before a month passed, Oakwood left Rebecca alone at the hotel while he traveled overnight on business. When he returned, he excitedly told Rebecca that he had a magnificent surprise for her. She would see it the following weekend.

Early Saturday morning, Rebecca and Oakwood boarded the train for the forty-mile trip on the recently opened rail connection from Albany, New York to West Stockbridge, Massachusetts. A brougham and driver met them at the station.

The carriage ride over dusty mountain roads was annoying to the pampered Rebecca but she dared not complain.

Oakwood assured Rebecca, "It isn't far now, my dear."

At the top of a steep incline, the road leveled. Oakwood tapped his walking stick on the coach roof, instructing the driver to stop. Hand in hand, Oakwood led Rebecca over a well-worn path to a clearing. The view was breathtaking, the height dizzying. Oakwood's firm hand directed Rebecca to the edge of the sheer cliff. Below, acres of meadows sprawled around a large farmhouse, surrounded by barns, an icehouse, stables, and paddocks. Remnants of a garden ringed a freshly painted, gleaming-white gazebo. Beyond the terraced plateau, a sunlit valley stretched to the horizon.

Oakwood announced, "There is our new home, my dear, isn't it beautiful?"

Confused, Rebecca turned to Oakwood, the silent question displayed on her face.

"Isn't it magnificent?" Oakwood's expression changed from delight to consternation, "This is our new home, a profitable dairy farm." He puffed his chest proudly, "The dairy business is a fine fit with the rest of my interests. I purchased it for us. We will raise our children here."

The dairy farm indeed promised to be a profitable venture for Oakwood, but the true motive for purchasing a secluded house was to sequester his new bride, whom he knew to be too generous with her charms. She was his property now.

Back in the carriage with Oakwood's heat pressed against her Rebecca asked, "When do you plan to move to this farm?"

"Today," Oakwood responded gruffly. "We are moving, to-day. Your personal belongings are coming with your new maid."

Rebecca was desolate but she knew this was not the time to protest. Did Oakwood plan to tyrannize her for the rest of her life?

Soon Rebecca would see her new prison, and meet the man who would steal her heart.

Chapter Three

May 1935

Marie squealed. "Un très beau paysage. Eet eez sooo beautiful, Zak-Kair-rie, the scenery. And za house, Une belle maison."

Zack crushed his petite wife with a loving hug, "It is a beautiful house."

One arm around Marie's waist, Zack, swept the view with his other and crooned, "C'est très magnifique. It is quite magnificent."

It was sunset and the couple basked in the reflection from the ridge.

Before purchasing the property, Marie knew this place would be important in her life. It was part of her destiny. The farmstead held an unexplainable attraction and the gazebo stirred feelings deep in Marie. She tried to describe what she felt to Zack, but it was beyond his understanding.

The legend of the ridge fascinated Marie, as did the contents of the locked antique chest. The key to the chest of memories passed by contract with the farm's deed to each new owner, Marie was titillated, looking forward to learning the special secrets both held.

Marie and Zack purchased the remote farm as a retreat; however, both entertained the thought of making it their permanent family home some day. Rail transportation was near enough for Zack's travel needs. Daily business communications consisted mostly of telegrams and mail. Marie and Zack could easily manage business affairs from an office at the farm. When that day arrived, they would maintain a small staff in their New York office, as well as their apartment in the city for social occasions.

Marie looked forward with excitement and impatient wonder to what the future held in store. She decided to rename their estate, Redemption Ridge Farm.

Chapter Four

Friday, December 21, 1990

6:59 a.m.

It began to snow. The small flakes dissolved quickly on the car's warm windshield and on the surface of the highway as Jonathan exited the Taconic Parkway, heading east on Interstate 90 into Massachusetts.

Under different circumstances, he would have canceled an appointment so far from home. Predictions of appreciable accumulation presented a concern; but the dictates of his meeting offered no alternative. It was too important to let a little snow interfere. He assured himself that road crews were prepared to deal with the storm.

Exiting the Mass Pike into the Berkshires, he found only wet rural roads. So far so good, Jonathan thought.

His car's dashboard clock glowed 7:40 a.m., as Jonathan drove into the picturesque New England town. He had time to stretch his legs and enjoy a hot breakfast at the cozy-looking diner on the main street.

The window edges of the restaurant wore cliché-canned frost. Jonathan had to smile as a three-foot tall Santa, rotating his hips in tune with a mechanical Ho, Ho, Ho, greeted him. The Formica and stainless steel interior offered a dated charm. As soon as the door closed behind him, the warmth of the restaurant embraced him, and smell of fresh brewed coffee and fried bacon wrapped him in comfort.

Perfect, Jonathan thought.

From behind the long counter, a pleasant-looking woman wearing an apron tied at the waist and fuzzy, reindeer antlers glanced at him over her shoulder. She was chatting with a customer. "Well what do you think?" She said slyly to the woman seated across the counter. The customer eyed the tall, lean, young man at the door and said, "Not Pittsfield or Springfield, maybe Albany or Boston."

The woman wearing the apron gave the new arrival a cursory evaluation. He was about thirty years old and neatly dressed. His clothes looked expensive, although not right for the weather. The short jacket hung open exposing a crisply pressed button down Oxford. His designer jeans wore a sharp crease. She straightened for duty. With half-turned head, she offered, "Judging by the way he's dressed I'll go with New York City."

Her customers enjoyed how accurately Midge could size-up a stranger as soon as they entered the restaurant.

Jonathan passed the vinyl booths by the frosted windows. He headed for a stationary, backless stool at the opposite end of the counter. Reindeer Antlers grabbed a coffee mug and a full pot of black brew and headed his way. She wore a bulky, Christmas Rudolph sweater. Watching her approach, Jonathan noted her boots were even fuzzier than her antlers and his grin stretched to a full smile, which she obviously appreciated.

"Morn'in mister," she said cheerily.

"Good morning," Jonathan croaked, the first time he had spoken since yesterday.

"Happy Holidays, name's Midge, what can I get for you?"

Before Jonathan could speak again, she pulled her sweater aside and pointed to the badge on her chest. "Short for Michelle, didn't think Michelle was a fit for this place, Midge kind of goes with the décor, don't you think?"

Jonathan bet she used the line on all her new customers. It worked. Jonathan immediately liked Midge.

"Studying the origin and meaning of names is a hobby of mine—Michelle is a very special name," Jonathan complimented, "but Midge seems to fit you well."

"Special name eh? Never looked it up, but I've been told it means something like looking like a goddess."

Not exactly, Jonathan thought, but he just smiled as Midge theatrically fluffed her hair in an exaggerated gesture of vanity.

"Michelle was very popular when I was born back in the forties." She wagged a finger and shook her head, "Don't ask how far back!

"Then in the seventies the Beatles made 'Michelle' popular again. Now there are all those under twenty-year-old chicks with the same name running around. That's about the only thing I have in common with them!"

Midge boldly asked, "What can I call you, mister?"

"Jonathan, Jonathan Dunquin."

"Well Jonathan Dunquin, it's a pleasure." She touched her pencil-holding finger to her fuzzy right antler. "Now, what'll you have?"

Midge took Jonathan's order and yelled it through an opening in the wall. A muffled male voice repeated it. Then she left the counter to attend to customers sitting in the booths. They all appeared to be regulars. She chatted and joked with each of them.

Jonathan made a mental note to include a description of the restaurant and Midge in his journalistic report of his New England visit.

Midge provided constant service and delivered Jonathan his order of juice, egg sandwich with extra bacon, and a side of home fries. She brought more cream and kept Jonathan's coffee cup brimming.

Before leaving him to consume the sugar, caffeine, and cholesterol-fix, Midge tilted her head to one side and stood back to study Jonathan. "Nice jacket," she said, referring to his unzipped, unlined designer jacket of buttery-tan leather.

"Thank you, it's waterproofed and it breaks the wind," Jonathan said somewhat embarrassed. In his foggy, early morning departure, he had forgotten his natty scarf, which together with the designer jacket, zipped tight, gave an illusion of warmth and comfort.

"Very fashionable, but it's too light for this weather," Midge persisted.

Jonathan's face flushed, "It's enough, and my car is warm."

Midge assumed a furrowed brow, "Let me guess, city boy; probably New York, college grad, good job. Here on business, right?"

"Guilty on all counts, am I that obvious?"

"Some folks think I'm psychic or something. Maybe I am. The stuff that comes to me usually is right on," Midge said proudly. She grinned somewhat sheepishly, "But, this time I was guessing. Yes, you are kind'a obvious. We see many city folks, especially New Yorkers but we don't see too many this time of year. I wouldn't venture a guess in the summer when all the folks are in shorts, flip flops, and printed tees."

Midge talked as Jonathan munched and sipped. She leaned her generous rear against the back counter and gave him a capsule view of life in a small Berkshire town, then turned to predict the weather. She seemed to think the storm would be worse than predicted. Midge said her bones told her more than the weatherman ever did. Jonathan hoped Midge's bones were wrong.

When Jonathan told her his destination, Midge's eyebrows disappeared behind her bangs and she bit her lower lip. "Well, now," she hesitated and a distracted look crossed her face. At first Midge felt happiness, in her mind's eye, the young man stood surrounded by color with a fair-haired woman by his side. Both glowed with mutual love.

Then, just as quickly, she felt fear. She saw the shadowed figure of a man she knew was Jonathan. He lay in the dark waiting for death. Midge tried blinking away the upsetting thought, but the young man's shocked, distorted face flashed again. This time she watched as he fought to correct his skidding vehicle.

Midge's facial contortions stopped Jonathan mid chew. He had a feeling of dread, "Is there a problem?" he asked.

"No, no, a stray thought just crossed my mind."

Midge recovered quickly and went on, "You're different from most that come to the Todd's. It's a horse breeding farm you know; you don't look like one of the horsy set."

From his years of experience interviewing people, something told Jonathan it was not the real reason for her reaction. A good recovery though, he thought, probably gained over her years of experience successfully removing her foot from her mouth. Jonathan had a nagging feeling Midge and he had connected on a different level.

Midge proceeded to give Jonathan directions. "The Todd place is easy enough to find. Head for the church down the street, then take the first right after the next traffic light, that's Ridge Lane. Follow it to where the paving ends; you'll see the driveway entrance."

Midge's directions matched those enclosed in the unexpected letter Jonathan received several weeks earlier.

"Do you know the Todds?"

"Knew the missus some, saw her a lot at church, came in here for lunch with friends occasionally. Very nice lady, she died a couple of years ago. Saw the mister at the funeral with their family. Don't think I've seen him since. Guess he is still alive. He must be pretty old."

Jonathan thought about the subject of his interview. Zacharie Todd was a nonagenarian billionaire and an entrepreneurial legend. He was also a recluse

Rumors of Todd's extreme generosity were unconfirmed. If true, he was a major charitable contributor and philanthropist.

"Midge, you seem to be an expert on this town. Redemption Ridge is an interesting name, do you know the background?"

"As the story goes, spirits must return to the base of the cliff for redemption."

Jonathan flashed a look of skepticism, but nodded to Midge to continue.

"Well, those committing suicide and murder must."

"There have been suicides and murders here?" Jonathan was incredulous.

Midge continued, "Desperate lovers jumped, cheating lovers were pushed, and some unfortunates just got dragged along by the spurned party.

"Of course, accidents also caused many deaths when the old road ran near the edge of the cliff, before it was moved back into the woods. The clearing that remained at the peak became a romantic place for lovers to meet and watch the sunset. It got the reputation of being a lover's leap.

"The ridge gives me the creeps; kind' a like it knows things. You will see how ominous it can be once you are in the lane. The cliff is sheer, straight top to bottom. In a certain light, from a distance, it looks like a man's face."

As Midge looked at Jonathan, her vision clouded then cleared. He was dressed differently and standing in a building without walls. Flowers hung in open frames. The woman Midge envisioned moments before was with him. The scene was beautiful, but it made Midge very sad.

Inhaling deeply, Midge squared her shoulders and returned to the moment.

Midge rolled her eyes and rocked her head back and forth. "Then there was the double murder and suicide at the farm, a shotgun shooting, back in the middle 1800s. The jealous husband returned from a business trip and caught his cheating wife and her lover in his bed. He blew both of them away then shot himself. I expect those three either have or will face Redemption Ridge penance."

"Penance?" Jonathan questioned.

"It's all about Karma. I think the word is East Indian, meaning consequences or something like that."

Jonathan smirked, "I know what Karma means, and it's when a person is held accountable for their actions in perpetuity. It is a belief of Hinduism and Buddhism."

Midge looked nettled and put both hands on her hips, her body language demanding an apology.

"Sorry, Midge, that was boorish of me."

Accustomed to customer repartee, Midge appeared quickly appeased, "Well with karma, a soul has a certain period after death for rest and reflection. During that time, it can revisit important places and people from its life and decide when and where to return in another human life. When the soul is ready, it comes back again."

"The actual term is transmigration and many believe the soul passes from one body to another at death."

Again, Midge scowled, hands on hips, "Do you want to hear my story about Redemption Ridge or don't you, Mr. Big City?"

Jonathan rocked back on the stool and raised both hands in front of his shoulders, "Okay, okay, I did it again, it was wrong to interrupt, you're right, it's your story."

Midge scowled briefly, "There is both positive and negative karma depending upon which the soul needs or has a right to experience.

"Now, negative karma is when the soul gets the opportunity to experience the same pain it caused in life and the chance to make it up to the injured party. It's like, do it right or do it over, repeatedly and painfully until you do.

"There is also positive karma. That is a rewarding life. This is also when a victim benefits from the ill-doer's making things right."

Midge assumed an affirmative expression. "Of course, that's the simple explanation; there are degrees of guilt involved. Anyway, there have been many reports of people seeing ghosts in the area and hearing horrible screams."

A cold chill went down Jonathan's spine. Trying to shrug off the feeling, he brought a scornful look to his face. "It is an interesting story, but you don't really believe it, do you? I don't believe in multiple lives, and I don't put any stock in the supernatural part."

Midge aimed a look that would melt ice at Jonathan, turned, and left to attend another customer. Jonathan finished his breakfast and Midge returned with his check.

Jonathan took a coffee for the road in a Styrofoam cup, paid the check and told Midge to keep the change. His generosity did not alter the concerned expression on Midge's face. It made Jonathan uneasy.

"Well, Mr. Jonathan-know-it-all-Dunquin, with this weather, you better drive carefully," Midge, said. The expression on her face and the foreboding comment raised the hair on the back of Jonathan's neck.

"I will, happy holidays, Midge." Jonathan stopped short of apologizing.

Midge forced a smile, "Happy holidays!" She strode back to the customer she had been talking to when Jonathan entered.

At the door the Santa chortled again, Jonathan turned to deliver a parting smile.

Midge returned the smile and nodded a fuzzy antler wag. She and her customer seemed to be sharing some secret. Jonathan suspected they were talking about him.

Chapter Five

Below the Ridge

As soon as she saw Jonathan's car pull away, Midge left the customer at the counter and went to the kitchen to talk to her husband, Jake, the cook.

"The young man who just left, the egg sandwich with extra bacon, I think he might be the one I saw in a vision several months ago. Remember, I told you, it came to me that someone with a special connection to the ridge and the farm would be in town around Christmas. His name is Jonathan and he is kind of a smart aleck pain in the butt, but I think deep down he is a good soul, just needs to do a little growing up."

Jake chomped on a carrot stick while giving Midge casual attention. "Babe, I have learned not to question anything you see, feel, or come out with. So, why do you feel he is so important?"

"While I was talking to him I saw things. I'm concerned for his safety. The visions came so quickly that I couldn't separate past, present, or future."

Acting as though he just noticed, Jake looked closely at Midge's fuzzy antlers. He took her in his arms and hugged her tenderly.

The snow was light when Jonathan left the restaurant. He shook off his jacket, placed it on the passenger seat, and rested the hot coffee in a holder on the car's console. The car held the warmth of the long morning drive and falling snow melted quickly on the windshield. He turned on the wipers and the radio.

Jonathan found Ridge Lane to be barely a path, narrow and winding with patches of gritty ice showing through the fresh cover. A pasture fence and an occasional utility pole crowded the lane on Jonathan's left, a precipitous slope rose quickly to his right. Rounding a bend, the slope stopped abruptly as though sliced by a giant knife. Jonathan leaned forward over the steering wheel, peering up, but unable to see the top. A feeling of panic overcame Jonathan, he felt claustrophobic.

What caused this reaction? Jonathan's mind searched for an answer. Was some chemical from the engine entering the car through the ventilation system? He cranked the driver's window all the way down to let in fresh air. The cold blast and wet snow made him close it quickly. He forced himself to think of something else.

His thoughts turned to the mysterious letter that brought him here. The letter arrived just after Thanksgiving. It was from a Manhattan attorney's office offering Jonathan an exclusive interview with Zacharie Todd. The appointment time, date and location were specific together with instructions to call Attorney West and confirm the appointment. When he read it, his heart jumped. It presented the opportunity of a lifetime for a journalist.

The firm's name on the letterhead looked familiar but Jonathan could not recall why. When he telephoned, Attorney West took his call immediately but would not answer any of his questions. She stressed the time and date of the appointment. It could not be changed. The attorney asked if Jonathan intended to accept the invitation as presented, yes or no. "Yes, of course," he said, without hesitation.

Jonathan recently resigned from a secure job with a business publication, striking out on his own as a freelance writer. With his car paid for, and money in the bank, it was not likely that he would starve. Very soon after leaving his job at the paper, the surprise interview invitation arrived. He could not guess how he qualified for such consideration. The letter said 'an exclusive interview,' Jonathan found it hard to believe his good fortune. Todd's story would be saleable. There could be a book in it.

Chapter Six

The Arrival

An explosion of dark fury erupted from Jonathan's left; he twisted the wheel in panic and slammed the brakes. The ten-year-old sedan slid broadside over hidden black ice. Finally, the tires gripped, halting the breathtaking skid abruptly. Jonathan's driver seat slammed forward and the steering wheel jammed painfully into Jonathan's groin. The Styrofoam cup toppled from its perch, splashing its steaming contents to the floor, the engine stalled, wipers pulsed, heater hummed, coffee pooled, the dash clock flipped to 8:41, and voices of the Westminster Choir singing, "The Holly and The Ivy," flowed from the car's FM.

Heart pounding, nerves vibrating, Jonathan sat in the stalled car his torso pinched by the steering wheel.

Recovering from the near collision took time. Slowly Jonathan felt for the seatbelt release. He clicked himself free and wrenched the seat ratchet back. Next, he salvaged his expensive jacket from the near miss of the coffee puddle on the passenger's side floor. He contemplated his painful groin, then turned off the radio and attempted to get his bearings.

The car was pointing in the right direction. Jonathan wiped the fogged driver-door window with a shirt-sleeved forearm. Startled, he gasped as a monstrous black apparition filled his view. A huge equine head swayed with flaring nostrils at the end of a thick-arched neck. The creature seemed to be laughing at him as Jonathan flinched with fear. It snorted froths of steam into the frigid air. Muscles quivered and hooves stomped. Glistening eyes bulged. Curled lips exposed large yellow teeth. The gigantic shaggy body leaned its bulk against the pasture fence.

Fighting panic, Jonathan tried to ignore the fearsome presence as he nervously twisted the key in the ignition. To his relief the stalled engine responded to his shaking fingers.

Jonathan fought the urge to race away. Feeling somewhat protected in his steel and glass capsule, he sat for several minutes, taking deep breaths, until his composure slowly returned.

Warily, under the watchful eye of the beast, Jonathan inched the car ahead onto the narrow path and continued to his destination.

Driving cautiously, Jonathan's low speed presented no challenge for his escort. The stallion paced the car nose to nose in an easy floating trot. He carried his proud head high on an extended neck. Jonathan guessed the animal weighed as much as his car. With each fluid step, the heavy winter coat bounced over thickly defined muscles. Jonathan swapped glances between the horse and lane, fascinated as the new snow puffed with the impact of each giant hoof. It was the first time Jonathan ever saw a horse as large or as black in the flesh. The animal was impressive.

Captivated by the magnificent horse Jonathan almost forgot the immense rock wall on his right. He drifted startlingly close and swerved away. Again, nausea swept over him. It must be all the fatty foods at breakfast, he thought, or too much coffee. He tried to shake off the feeling.

Ahead on his left, Redemption Ridge Farm's sign swung gently over the arched entry. The driveway flared and the fence angled to allow a large truck or trailer to make a wide turn. The road continued beyond the entry, unpaved and rutted. Cables from the last utility pole terminated at a small building.

It was a relief to have the cliff wall behind him as Jonathan passed under the sign. Fenced pastures spread on both sides of the driveway, a serene picture freshly clad in white.

At the top of a rise, farm buildings came into view. The fence on his left cut away and disappeared behind an antique farmhouse.

Jonathan's enormous companion bucked and kicked in apparent delight and thundered off.

Despite the storm-caused darkness, the setting was beautiful contrasted with the fresh snow. The rambling two-story lay to the left and the driveway continued to wrap around stately barns and stables. Wreaths and swags of fresh pine boughs hung on the facing windows of the house.

A large Victorian gazebo caught Jonathan's attention and the sight thrilled him. A gated picket fence surrounded the structure.

The emotional maelstrom of the past few minutes brought on sudden fatigue. Jonathan stopped several yards from the house. He tilted his head back. With the engine idling out of gear, the humming heater's warmth gently soothed him.

It had been a stressful morning. Jonathan began his day with apprehension over the important appointment. His predawn departure from the city, hours of highway driving, and the shocking encounter on the lane contributed to his anxiety. Nerves, he thought, too much caffeine.

Jonathan's mind drifted. He imagined a bright azure sky behind a lacy veil of young leaves on towering trees. A harmony of spring fragrances filled him with a sense of well-being. He enjoyed the rapture as long as he could before his internal clock signaled.

Reluctantly, Jonathan opened his eyes and scanned the clock. "Time to go to work," he put the car in gear and drove as close as possible to the front steps.

Naked silhouettes of oaks and maples stood guard around the house as they loyally had for decades, their branch forks gathering falling flakes. Dark stalks poked from winter-shredded gardens. Jonathan imagined other seasons with colorful life and fragrances.

How strange it is to be thinking of flowers in a winter storm, he thought.

This was his first visit but it all seemed so familiar. The well-maintained house tilted and twisted with age. The front porch was deep; a large picture window on one side of the house faced meadows and pastures. Three slabs of snow-capped red stone served as the front steps.

The house was big, but not what Jonathan expected. His pre-arrival vision of Zacharie Todd's home was of a mansion surrounded by high walls with a guarded entry. After all, the man had to be a billionaire.

Despite his searching, the only archive photos of Todd Jonathan he found were over twenty years old, strange for a man with such achievements. If the few stories written in past decades bore any truth, Zacharie Todd faced and overcame challenges that would have stopped most men.

As a teenager, Todd served in the army during World War I. He started a successful wine import business before he was twenty-two. Todd amassed a personal fortune from a variety of interests by the time he was thirty. He survived Prohibition, the Great Depression and World War II's U-Boat impact on the European shipping to America. He lost everything at one time, recovered and rebuilt his empire again, all the time avoiding the public eye. Todd seemed to be a human incarnation of the Golden Phoenix. Yet, he was able to remain a phantom.

8:58 a.m.

Jonathan pressed his forehead against the cold glass and peered up at the house. A shadow moved in a second-floor window. Good, he thought, they know I'm here. He turned off the engine and took a deep breath.

Jonathan swung out of the car and hit the frigid air of the gray New England morning. It was getting colder and the snow was heavier. Shivering, he tugged on the light jacket and cursed himself again for forgetting his scarf. He wrestled his well-worn brief case from behind the seat where it had become wedged. Zipping up with gloveless hands, he gave a mournful look at the coffee covered carpet, slammed the driver's door with his heel, and hurried to the house. He skipped the front steps to the porch and bounced the large brass knocker.

Next to the door mounted on the red clapboard was a plaque, *Circa 1805*. With fingers quickly numbing, he bounced the knocker a second, then a third time. Still no response, "Great," he heard himself say aloud, and then tested the door handle. A twist with a slight push and the door opened enough for Jonathan to bend his upper body inside.

The house was warm and quiet except for the loud ticking of an impressive grandfather clock standing by the front door. The sweet odor of stale pipe smoke blended with the faint smell of wood burning in a fireplace. Jonathan called out, "Hello, I'm the writer from New York here to interview Mr. Todd." He stepped in and closed the door.

There were no lights burning in the shadow-filled house. Jonathan called out again, no response.

From the entry foyer, Jonathan could see into three rooms and a hall beyond. The furnishings were an eclectic blend of expensive American, European, and Asian antiques. Oriental carpets lay on age-darkened, polished wood floors. Quaint print paper tastefully covered the walls, interrupted occasionally by museum quality art. Fine porcelains and expensive bronze statues stood carefully placed in étagère and on pedestals.

Jonathan peered into a proper library where embers glowed in the glass-enclosed fireplace, an indication someone would soon return. The décor was English Club. Hunter-green, supple leather chairs flanked the fireplace. In a space carved from the bookcases, on the opposite wall, nestled a matching leather love seat under a handsomely framed print of James Pillar's Hyde Park Corner.

To the right of one chair, Jonathan recognized an antique smoking stand with built-in humidor and pipe racks. On the chair, a folded pair of reading glasses perched on a worn copy of Clavell's Nobel House waiting for its reader to return.

Jonathan considered settling into the empty overstuffed chair to enjoy the warmth and wait. He looked around the magnificent room. The occupants of the tall shelves lining the walls drew him. One bookcase contained jewels of leather-bound first editions, classic novels, and books of poetry. Other shelves promised equal treasures. Jonathan thought how much he would enjoy spending time in this room. As fate would have it, he would!

Turning to the door to leave, a feeling of déjà vu gripped Jonathan. Something felt so familiar, not the furniture, the oriental carpets, or the museum quality art. A fragrance mixed with the smoky odors, with it came a joyful feeling of anticipation. Jonathan quickly returned to the hall, expecting to see a young woman descending the stairs. There was no one.

"Am I hallucinating?"

Dejected, Jonathan looked into each of the rooms. Glancing through a window, he saw a light in a nearby building and decided to investigate. The shadow in the second-floor window must have been a trick of light or his imagination.

Ignoring the lack of protection of his light jacket and missing scarf, Jonathan left the warm farmhouse, the barn showed the only sign of life.

Jonathan's leather-soled dress shoes slipped in the fresh snow. He made it with short, shuffling steps. Balancing awkwardly, with his briefcase in one hand, it took his full 175 pounds on his six-foot-one frame to slide the massive door open enough to squeeze through. Closing the door from the dry floor inside was a bit easier.

The familiar and agreeable odors of horse, hay, and fresh cedar greeted Jonathan. They brought back another memory when a Central Park stable had played a role in his recent, albeit short-lived, summer romance.

Her name was Priscilla. She was an attractive and well-endowed equestrian. Priscilla introduced Jonathan to riding and equine nomenclature. He felt that the best way to impress her was to show an interest in her horseback riding hobby. Remembering brought a grin to Jonathan's cold, stiff face. Her equitation was as impressive as her symmetry. Riding with her was painful to his derriere but fulfilling to his libido. Try as he could, Jonathan could not correct his unimpressive saddle bounce.

The handsome riding instructor obsessed about Priscilla's form and coarsely criticized Jonathan's "seat," as he called it. One day, adding to Jonathan's backside bruises, came the ego crushing coup de grâce. Priscilla, his voluptuous riding companion, rode off into a hazy New York sunset with the handsome riding instructor.

Such had been the history of Jonathan's love life. However, that might change soon. Friends in the city were acting as business agent and Cupid. Jonathan's friend, Sue, worked with a woman who was looking for a ghostwriter to finish her deceased husband's memoirs. The woman's unmarried daughter was about Jonathan's age. Sue and her husband Jeff arranged a pre Christmas dinner party, so all could meet. Jonathan was very much looking forward to the gathering.

Bearing down on thirty, Jonathan felt that the bachelor life should end. He made a good living and invested cautiously. An MBA from Wharton, together with meeting the right people at college, helped him in his move to New York City and a respectable position with a weekly business paper; his first and only employer since college. He started as a research assistant and quickly moved to the position of associate editor.

Moving to the world's melting pot was an unnerving culture shock for the Midwesterner. He acclimated, but the demands of his job allowed little time for socializing. Jonathan craved a normal life and someone special to share it. Freelancing seemed the thing to do. It would allow the opportunity to write more about people and less about mergers and acquisitions. Developing his personal life was the goal, so Jonathan left the paper.

Earl, the editor and Jonathan's boss, was not encouraging. He told Jonathan he had gotten to know two Jonathan Dunquins; one, the journalist—disciplined, careful, thoughtful, and professional; the personal—brash, snide, insensitive, and self-centered. Earl made a point that Jonathan's future and personal success warranted areas of evaluation and adjustment.

With this opportunity, today, Jonathan would be Jonathan Dunquin the disciplined, professional journalist. Improving on the other Jonathan would take time.

Jonathan's entry started a commotion among the equine occupants. Dark heads emerged on both sides of the wide aisle, each
puffing steam into the cool stable. Huge eyes flashed white as they
strained to see the visitor. Discordant sounds of snorting and guttural snickering greeted him. Hoofs bumped stall doors and
thumped dully on wood-chip bedded floors. Equipped with several tons of live heaters, the stable was warmer than outside.

The structure's interior showed the patina of age. Posts pet-
rified by decades supported equally stout, hand-hewn beams,
dovetailed where they joined. The rodent patrol in the form of
two plump felines dozed on top of a grain bin. Both curled with
bushy tails across the other's nose, the fluffy black and white
showed a momentary interest by opening one eye. The other cat
feigned disinterest.

Jonathan jumped as something bumped his thigh. A dark
brown retriever was sniffing Jonathan's leg. The dog turned and
sauntered to a pile of blankets.

"You must be the writer," the voice rang with a bell-like resonance. The old man gestured to Jonathan to approach, then
turned his attention to a giant horse.

Chains attached to either side of a leather halter held the animal perpendicular to Jonathan and one eye seemed to glare at
Jonathan. Closer he did not want to be.

Jonathan looked expectantly at a darkened window with the
word "Office" in the corner. "I'm here to interview Mr. Todd.
Mr. Zacharie Todd. Is he here?"

The man turned again to face Jonathan, he looked amused,
"I'm Zack Todd."

"Come back here so we don't have to shout at one another."

Horses did not frighten Jonathan in the past, but this one did.
He stood at least six foot six inches at the withers, where his neck
and muscular back met. His size diminished Todd. When he
raised his head, it towered over the man.

Todd coaxed a front leg of the big animal up and began
scraping the hoof with a tool. The leg probably weighed as much
as Jonathan did. With the horse's help, the man steadied the hoof

against his own thigh and leaned into the horse's body. Jonathan knew the horse participated in the procedure by lifting and holding its leg up. It was another lesson learned from his Central Park riding experience. With bitterness, Jonathan recalled the handsome riding instructor's excessive attention to the well-built Priscilla while Jonathan cared for the horse he had ridden without assistance.

The old man patted the big horse with the cue to put the finished leg down.

"Well come on back," Todd said as he moved to the stallion's rump. The big black lifted his leg, responding to another pat and voice command.

Impossible, Jonathan thought. This could not be the subject of his interview. This man certainly did not look ninety years old. This man was wiry, moving with confidence. Not the feeble old soul Jonathan expected to find wrapped in a shawl and sitting in a rocker.

Zacharie Todd lowered the last of the cleaned hoofs. He slapped the animal's neck, an indication of appreciation to the horse, and then turned to study Jonathan from under the brim of a faded Red Sox cap.

"I'm here to do the interview," Jonathan said slowly moving toward the man and animal.

"I know," the old man said with a crooked grin. He unsnapped the crossties and bullied the big animal into an oversized stall, close to where Jonathan stood. He closed the stall door and threw a heavy bolt into its housing. The big black head poked out and Jonathan jumped in retreat, his reaction caused the nonagenarian to chuckle.

With the two men closer, Jonathan could see the signs of age, jerky movement, craggy face, body a bit stooped.

Todd grinned brightly, removed one glove, and extended his hand in greeting. Standing a full head shorter than Jonathan did not affect his formidability. His face was thin and weathered with a sharp chin and a wide, steel-gray mustache. The mischievous grin periodically flashed over his face and one corner of his mouth twitched slightly. Steel-blue eyes twinkled from behind dusty, rimless glasses. His penetrating gaze made Jonathan self-conscious and uncomfortable. Could the old man read Jonathan's mind? Could he know about the New York stable, Priscilla, and the handsome riding instructor?

"Jonathan Dunquin. Jonathan," he repeated and shook the extended hand nervously. He pulled out his handkerchief and wiped his running nose. Stamping cold feet, he asked, "Can we go into the house Mr. Todd? I'm not really dressed for this weather."

"No you're not, are you. Where are your gloves and hat?" Todd eyed Jonathan's jacket with a twisted smile.

"That jacket isn't worth a damn," he said, displaying a sly sense of humor.

"I'll be finished here in a few minutes. I would have you wait in the office but the heat is not on. Cozy up to one of the horses," he chuckled, "they will keep you warm. And, call me Zack."

Now Jonathan knew he was kidding. The old man continued to snicker as he slowly climbed steep stairs into the hayloft. He wrestled two large bales of hay to the edge above Jonathan.

"Stand clear, when I drop these, they'll bounce."

The heavy bales hit the barn floor puffing clouds of dust. Jonathan jumped back. The noise and the hay on the barn floor startled and excited the horses. They snorted, and bumped the stall walls. Jonathan appreciated the heavy oak that separated them.

Something was happening to Jonathan. The sounds and smells surrounding him triggered an out-of-body feeling and a rush of pleasure. A bright summer day spilled through the open barn door and a woman glided toward him. She wore a translucent dress that silhouetted her youthful form. As she came closer, Jonathan felt breathless. Her face radiated love; she carried the summer sky in her eyes, sunlight shimmered from her hair. Jonathan knew she planned to kiss him as she handed him a fragrant bouquet.

As Jonathan reached for the bouquet, something snapped. He was back in the darkened barn. Zack had switched off the overhead lights. The gloom made it feel colder and Jonathan felt hollow.

"That will keep these guys happy for a while. We can go into the house now. How was the drive from the city?" Todd's voice cut the air.

"Fine," Jonathan stuttered, "fine, no problems."

The sounds of munching mixed with restless movement and the fragrances of fresh hay. Hoping for the warm vision to return, Jonathan thought, I don't want to leave.

"Let's go warm you up with a hot coffee. You drink coffee, don't you, Jonathan Dunquin?" Zack asked.

"Sometimes too much and sometimes not quickly enough," Jonathan muttered, thinking of his morning jitters and stained car carpet.

Showing measured good balance Zack rolled open the heavy barn door on its tracks with relative ease and moved briskly toward the house. Neither of the cats stirred. The brown dog jogged by the old man's side.

Slipping and sliding, Jonathan struggled to close the door. The snow, now ankle deep got into his shoes and melted quickly, soaking his thin socks.

Zack was about twenty-five feet ahead. He was talking softly to the dog. The alert canine watched his master's face intently as though reading his lips.

"What do you think, Homer?" Zack whispered. "Have we done the right thing? He seems like a fine young man, but what about his common sense. Coming to a farm in a snowstorm dressed like Saturday night in Miami. Did you see those shoes? I'll bet you the trimmings of a steak they have leather soles. He'll likely be on his keister soon." The attentive retriever issued a guttural woof of agreement, then snapped at the annoying snowflakes.

Doing his newly learned short slide shuffle, Jonathan avoided near falls, and finally caught up with Zack and the dog. He noticed the sidelong smirk that passed the old man's face.

Jonathan rolled his head upward, narrowing his eyes against the stinging, swirling ice crystals.

Zack said, "It's going to be a big one."

"Hope not," Jonathan muttered, thinking of his drive back to the city. I had better get this interview over fast.

"You might get snowed in here," Zack said with his underlying chuckle.

No way, Jonathan grumbled silently to himself. He shuddered as his gaze fell on the faint shadow of the snow-shrouded ridge face in the distance, and the acid taste of his breakfast bacon returned to Jonathan's throat. He scanned his surroundings and this time was chilled by the sight of the snow-covered garden and gazebo. Approaching the house from this perspective, the scene still seemed familiar, but now it was distressing.

Chapter Seven

Back in the Farmhouse

Inside the appreciated warmth of the mudroom, Zack peeled off gloves and hat. He shook off his heavy jacket hanging it near others on a hook by the back door. Jonathan shook snow from his shoes and wiped them with an old towel Zack provided. He used another towel to absorb the wet snow from his expensive jacket, examining the protection of the water repellent treatment that cost him extra. Thankfully, the waterproofing treatment worked. He hung the light jacket on the back of a nearby chair.

Zack stepped out of his work boots and into a pair of leather clogs. He produced a string mop from a closet and quickly whisked it around the wet floor.

Jonathan looked on, and thought about his cold feet, "Is it alright for me to take off my shoes and socks so they can dry?"

"Next time you come to a farm in a snowstorm you will know how to dress. Check the boot box. My sons and grandsons leave their farm clothing here. There are probably some laundered athletic socks—there may be clogs or slippers that will fit."

Wearing bright white woolen socks with purple stripes and pea-green chenille bedroom slippers, Jonathan placed his wet footwear near a heat register and followed Zack into a magnificent kitchen.

"The clogs didn't fit," Jonathan offered.

Zack paid no attention to Jonathan's colorful footwear; he turned on the lights and went to a Monson Maine sink that appeared to be over a hundred years old. He rinsed and wiped his glasses. Noting Jonathan's interest, he invited the journalist to look around.

The kitchen displayed a mix of antiquity and high end gourmet appliances. Jonathan admired the slate counter tops, the retro 60-inch O'Keefe & Merritt Vintage Gas Range and guessed that there was a Sub Zero Refrigerator hidden in the exquisitely fine cabinetry.

"This kitchen is perfect," Jonathan said.

"Are you a cook, Jonathan?"

"Out of necessity at first—living alone for so many years, then it became a hobby, now it is a passion."

"I'm a fair cook myself, but the kitchen was my wife Marie's doing. She designed it and she made wonderful things happen here."

The brown dog bumped against Jonathan's leg. Jonathan stooped to scratch a floppy ear with one hand while stroking the gleaming enamel of the stove with the other.

"What's the dog's name?" Jonathan asked.

"Homer." Zack replied.

"Homer, as in the *Iliad* and the *Odyssey*? He doesn't look like a poet," Jonathan joked feebly.

"No, Jonathan, 'Homer,' as in heading for home, his food, and bed. I'm not that intellectual, neither is the dog."

Hearing his name, Homer turned and walked slowly to Zack.

Jonathan wandered into the adjoining dining room and stood in front of the large picture window. Zack followed. "The snow is hiding the views today," Zack said. "On clear days we can see the valley floor in the distance to the west. The face of the ridge is over to the east. Our pastures and meadows terrace down from the ridge face. We have magnificent sunsets and at the golden hour, the sun reflects off the ridge. It is a truly spectacular sight.

Before we bought this place, the real estate agent arranged for us to stay for the sunset and we were sold."

"I'm trying to get my bearings," Jonathan said. "When I drove into town I came down a steep grade. On Ridge Lane, it seemed like I doubled back around the mountain."

"Good sense of direction, Jonathan. You came down from the ridge into town, and then circled the cliff face to come here. The road that brought you into town comes over the peak from the highway. You don't get the valley view from the top because of the tree line," Zack explained. "At one time that road ran along the edge of the ridge cliff but it was too dangerous. It was moved back, into the woods, many years ago."

At the mention of the ridge road, Jonathan's stomach turned over and he again tasted his greasy breakfast.

Turning to the room, Jonathan realized Zack had put on more lights. He had not looked into this room earlier. It was neat with thoughtful decorating touches and a feminine influence. Zack guessed the young writer's thoughts. "Most of the pretty things here are thanks to my Marie. She was the one with taste," he said soulfully.

An open arch led to a small sitting room. Zack entered, switched on table lamps, a desk lamp, and a portrait light. "This was Marie's favorite room," Zack said, "her retreat."

The room wore a comfortable décor of quiet elegance.

Jonathan guessed that a closed armoire standing against the wall behind the pecan desk housed a computer. A French impressionistic street scene hung over it.

"That looks like Paris," Jonathan said, referring to the copy of Camille Pissarro's *Avenue de l'Opers.*"

"It is a hand-painted copy of a Pissarro original painted after Haussmann's renovation of Paris. Marie loved it. It reminded her of her youth and of our many visits together to the city."

An illuminated oil painting of an exotic looking woman hung over a Delft-tiled fireplace. The woman appeared fresh and vibrant with an all-knowing smile. Her presence was so powerful Jonathan expected she would enter the room at any moment

"That's my Marie," Zack whispered reverently. It seemed appropriate for the quiet and somehow spiritual atmosphere. Jonathan turned to look at Zack, "She is beautiful."

"She is younger there, but she was just as beautiful before she died.

"Marie thought I was foolish keeping the old portrait on display and even tried once to hide it from me. However, I persisted and she finally allowed me to hang it in our bedroom. Marie passed in 1987. After she died, I moved the painting here. I come in to visit with her every day.

"I had that portrait of Marie painted while we were in Paris, back in the late 1940s. I thought; Paris, artists, you know. They say only a live artist can capture the true essence, the life of another human. A camera cannot do that. A camera can only capture the moment. I think that is true. There is my Marie! Now you know her. To me she never changed. The love still burned in the old man's eyes.

"We were married for sixty-five years, longer than many people live. They were wonderful years."

"I'm sorry. It must be difficult," Jonathan said.

The old man thrust back his shoulders. He studied Jonathan for a moment, "Jonathan, my new friend, you have no idea." He closed his eyes and smiled a warm closed mouth smile.

"I always feel her close," Zack continued, "so many beautiful memories. I miss her more than anyone can imagine, and I have shed many tears. We were inseparable. We even thought like one person."

Jonathan was at a loss for words.

At 10:02 a.m., the two men returned to the kitchen. Jonathan set his battered briefcase by the kitchen table leg. He turned a chair and straddled it, then took out the small tape recorder to get on with the interview.

Zack opened a cabinet and exposed the handsome refrigerator Jonathan suspected of hiding there. He removed a pan and placed it in one of the ovens. Then he shook coffee beans from a canister into a hand grinder.

"Mr. Todd, I really appreciate this opportunity. You can be sure I will do my best to justify your trust. May I ask how you happened to choose me for this interview? Many notable journalists would give an arm for this chance. TV networks would pay handsomely for a live interview with you.

His back to Jonathan, Zack clamored in a cupboard and spoke without turning, "Call me Zack, and let's drop the malarkey.

"To begin with, I did not plan this interview. My wife encouraged it before she died. There is nothing special about my life or me. My success came as much from being in the right place at the right time. Luck, played a big part, it is beyond me that anyone is interested in my experiences or my opinions. Chances are most people will disagree with my opinions anyway.

"As far as TV is concerned, I do not need money and I do not want to be the prize of some over-groomed actor pretending to be a journalist. Then there is the editing, and changing the meaning of what a person says.

"Are you going to twist my words, Jonathan?"

Jonathan gulped, "No. Absolutely not, anything you tell me will be presented straightforward I promise."

Zack faced Jonathan, the old man's shoulder quivering with delight, "Relax my boy; I'm just having fun with you. We'll have our coffee and get to know each other a little better, and then you can start your interview."

The smell of fresh ground coffee filled the air. Zack ground the beans and brewed the best coffee Jonathan ever tasted. It seemed that was all Zack would say on the subject of Jonathan's selection. Jonathan made a mental note to ease back into it later.

While the two men made small talk, fragrances from the oven and the fresh, brewed coffee filled the kitchen. Zack encouraged Jonathan to drink the steaming liquid black. He explained the recipe of his personal blend using coffee beans from places in the world Jonathan had never heard of.

Homer lay on the floor, following Zack's movements with his eyes. When Zack approached the range, Homer became alert and sniffed the air. Using dishtowel-wrapped hands, Zack reached into the magnificent oven and removed a hot pan of giant scones, which he transferred to a waiting basket on the table. Homer trotted along expectantly, and then sat patiently next to Zack's empty chair.

From the cabinet-camouflaged Sub Zero refrigerator Zack produced a small tub of something Jonathan never tasted before.

Zack puffed with pride. "It's Devonshire Cream, genuine English clotted cream. I learned how to make it from an English Dairyman on one of my trips. Do you like it?"

"Wow! Yes! How is it made?" Jonathan exclaimed around a mouthful.

"First, you'll need unpasteurized cream. That's the most difficult part. You let it stand for several hours before sterilizing it. To sterilize it, let it sit without boiling over very low heat for several more hours. After a slow pre-boiling process it has to stand again for several more hours." Zack struck a scholarly pose and said with authority, the time differs in winter and summer of course. Then it has to be stored again for another several hours. After that, thick cream forms on the surface and you skim it off. That's Devonshire cream."

While he spoke, Jonathan shamelessly lathered two scones with the rich cream and mixed the preserves Zack provided, a different one on every bite.

With another full mouth Jonathan asked, "Zack, did you really make this yourself?"

Zack grinned widely as he rewarded Homer's patience. "Of course not, I buy it at a specialty grocery store in Albany. Making it is a ridiculous amount of work and a terrible waste of time."

Zack's clear voice seemed to bend just right for effect. Jonathan nodded, "You got me," and stuffed his mouth with another clotted cream-smothered scone topped with preserves while Zack displayed his twisted grin.

"Wiping his face and rubbing his belly Jonathan asked, "Have you heard the local weather? I'd like to get back to the city before the roads get too bad."

"They're bad already; I think you might want to consider staying, now that you're here."

"I'm not prepared for an overnight and I have an important appointment back in the city…" Oh, oh, Jonathan thought, that was the wrong thing to say.

"An 'important appointment,' one that is more important than my interview?" Zack said sharply, his face hardening as he tilted back in his chair.

Jonathan fumbled for the right words. "Of course not, that came out wrong. I planned to drive back today because I had no reason to believe I couldn't."

Homer sensed the annoyance in the exchange and slunk back to his favorite corner.

Jonathan stalled to regain his composure. He waited for the heat to drain from his face and awkwardly pretended a search in his briefcase. "I'm still confused about the letter I received last month. It didn't explain anything—just directions here, today's date and the time for our meeting. Don't get me wrong, it is a great honor to be here. Just that the attorney was no help. She wouldn't answer my questions or tell me any more."

"She was doing what an attorney should do, complying with her client's wishes," Zack said sternly.

"How would you even know that I existed? Have we ever met before?"

"No."

"Do you know anything about me?"

Zack sat straight. Leaning toward the table, he looked Jonathan in the eye, his voice low and serious, "As a matter of fact, Jonathan, I have been aware of you for more than a dozen years."

This was nearly impossible. That would go back to my teens. There was nothing exceptional about my life, Jonathan thought. He could not imagine what might have drawn the attention of someone in Todd's position. Could this be a mistake? Did Todd and his attorney think he was someone else? The thought gripped his stomach like an icy fist.

"I don't understand."

"Are you the Jonathan Dunquin that attended Penn State and Wharton?" Zack asked.

Jonathan jerked back as the realization struck him, there was only one inference in the old man's comment, and it suddenly occurred to Jonathan why the New York law firm's name was familiar. They administrated the trust that paid Jonathan's full scholarships. He heard his own voice rise, "You—you paid for my education? Why, I don't understand?"

The corner of Zack's mouth twitched, "Well, not me, you are one of many recipients underwritten by a trust that Marie and I started years ago. We liked to find good young talent and make sure that talent isn't wasted. We enjoyed watching our protégés grow—from the wings, so to speak."

"But a full scholarship, that was very generous. I'm overwhelmed. I don't know what to say. Saying thank you doesn't seem like enough!" Jonathan's brain was trying to process this information in light of the circumstances of the meeting. He began to suspect that there was a motive connected to this interview that could prove uncomfortable. He tried to appear calm. "What could have impressed you about me while I was in high school? I mean my grades were good, but…" he trailed off.

"Do you remember a young woman by the name of Becky Baron?" Zack asked.

"Yes, she was a year ahead of me in high school, a very smart and popular girl. All the guys in our high school were crazy about her. We had a pet name for her. We called her 'The Bs.'"

"The bees, what did that mean?" Zack looked puzzled.

Jonathan felt his face redden with heat, "It was an expression of admiration. The letter 'B,' plural, it stood for blonde, blue eyes, beautiful, and brilliant." Jonathan tactfully left out bosomed.

An "oh really" look crossed Zack's face, his eyes narrowed, "Becky is my granddaughter. She matured quickly."

"Where is she now?"

Zack sucked in a breath with a look of exasperation.

"Becky is a physicist in a California think-tank. She went to

Stanford," it was as though the word brought a bad taste to Zack's mouth.

"I wanted her to go to an Ivy-League School, but Becky always knew what she wanted and got it."

"Stanford is a great school."

"Yes, and Becky is a very smart young woman; but I hoped that she would train for joining the family business. Well, maybe some day." Zack slumped back in his chair.

Homer's movement caught their attention. He was lying in front of the French doors to the patio when a rabbit hopped up to examine its reflection in the glass. Homer growled and stiffened, rising quickly. The frightened rabbit bounded away.

Homer cast a bored look back at the laughing men, stretched, and settled back into sentry position.

Brightening, Zack said, "It was Becky who suggested Marie and I give you special consideration. She was concerned that your financial circumstances might limit your potential."

Jonathan slid to the edge of his chair, "I didn't think Becky even knew my name. She was right though, times were tough for my family. The scholarship was part of a double blessing in our household."

Zack tilted his head, "You worked a full-time job nights and weekends while you were in high school, and continued to work and send money to your family while you attended college. That impressed Marie, Becky, and me."

How do Becky and Zack know so much about me? Where is this going? Jonathan thought.

"My family needed the money; my youngest sister Penny suffered from pediatric cancer." Jonathan said. "Treatment was very expensive and Mom quit her job to take care of Penny. My folks wanted to help me with college tuition but without the scholarship that would not have been possible. Penny's medical expenses were very high. They needed my help. Then my family got a break, financially. About the same time the scholarship came out of the blue."

Jonathan stared silently at the pen he twisted between his fingers. He remembered well how he felt about his family's circumstances while he was in high school. He was a teenager burning with anger. There were times he hated his sick sister. She received all the attention and the cost of her medical care meant that Jonathan had to do without. Before the scholarship and surprise medical aid came along, Jonathan lived with the thought that he would never go to college, trapped in a dead-end job for the rest of his life. His anger drove him, but he hid it well. Jonathan thought about the crappy jobs he took and the long hours he worked to contribute to the financial support of the family. He gave up a teenager's social life, using his few available waking hours to study in order to keep his grades up.

During Penny's last days, when she had to be hospitalized Jonathan paid his regular obligatory late night visit. He remembered the antiseptic smell and the cold halls echoing his approach to his sister's room. The staff greetings were subdued. Penny recognized her big brother's footfalls and beamed as he entered her room. Her sunken eyes widened and her mouth turned up in a smile for the brother she loved. She was so tiny and so pale surrounded by the big hospital bed. At that moment, Jonathan's heart melted. He wanted to hide from his shame and plead for Penny's forgiveness. Dropping to his knees, he buried his face in the covers and cried. Penny's frail hand stroked his head lovingly.

Zack looked at the floor until he felt Jonathan was ready to speak again.

"Becky and Marie thought that you might not go to college and would continue working to help provide for your sister's needs."

Zack's words brought Jonathan back to the farm's kitchen.

"As it happened, the doctors made some arrangement through St. Jude's that relieved much of the financial pressure. I was able to leave for college. It was a blessing for us all."

"My Marie was an angel. She watched the educational and the healing process of every young person who entered our lives and we chatted about individuals often, when she was alive. She told me then, and Becky reminded me recently, that you were a very special young man in high school and might be lost without help. Then, later, through the years, Marie developed a particular interest in you that I can't say I understood. It had something to do with her belief that you were very special. She kept her reasons cloaked in mystery. I never tried to understand Marie's intuitive side so we never visited her reasons."

"You paid full tuition through a graduate degree for me and you paid for Penny's care? All that came from you and Marie; strangers we never met?" Jonathan could no longer control his emotions, his eyes filled with tears as he stated what he now knew to be fact.

Zack's voice dropped to a whisper. "I understand you lost Penny a few years ago," he said, still looking at the floor.

"She was only twelve. She gave it a good fight. She lived a lot longer than the doctors thought she would. I guess that's thanks to you." Jonathan's voice caught several times as he answered.

Zack cleared his throat. "Losing a loved one is difficult, something we never get over."

This is no mistake, Jonathan thought, Zack knows exactly who I am, and he is still interested in my life, but why.

Controlling his emotions, Jonathan said, "You were starting to tell me how it happened that you selected me for this interview."

Zack leaned toward Jonathan, his voice low, "Let's get something straight young man. I have watched different emotions cross your face. I have seen doubt and suspicion. You are not being used, if that is what you think. You do not owe me anything and I assure you that I do not intend to exploit you or your family.

"I have become a pragmatist of the highest order because of life experiences. That fact has not altered my respect for every human being. Neither does it stop me from avoiding folks who do not respect others. I choose who I help.

"Marie and Becky planned the details of this interview between you and me years ago. According to Becky, it was postponed many times. Marie gave specific instructions to Becky to keep tabs on you.

"Becky called me a couple of months ago and told me she thought the time was right and that she would instruct my attorney to contact you and set things up. When I asked why, she only said she was following Mémère Marie's direction. That was good enough for me.

"I did some checking of my own however. Oh, by the way, your old boss, Earl, holds you in high regard although he seems to think that you soured while employed with him."

Jonathan thought, come on, another connection, where will this end?

With renewed annoyance, Jonathan blurted, "Let me guess, you also own the business paper. You're the publisher and Earl's boss."

"At one time I was, years ago. Now I am only a member of the board of directors."

As appreciative as he knew that he should be, Jonathan bordered on anger.

"You said Becky knew I was working at the paper. Did she or Marie have anything to do with my getting the job there?" Jonathan's voice betrayed his feeling.

"No, you got that on your own."

The old man was quiet for a few moments.

He sipped coffee, after a few seconds he spoke so quietly Jonathan strained to hear.

"Whatever else you might be thinking let me assure you that I am doing this only because it was Marie's wish. You were important to Marie and she shared her feeling with Becky. Marie paid attention to intuition. I trusted her. She was very sensitive in ways that I could never explain. She knew things; predicted events."

Leaning back in his chair, Zack continued, "Marie had a special connection with this farm. She often said that our being here was important to the happiness of so many souls and that we should feel blessed.

"Before Marie died, she told me that one day Jonathan Dunquin would answer my invitation and visit the farm. She said it would be arranged by Becky and made me promise that once the day and time of our appointment was set, it would not be changed under any circumstances.

"Now I suppose that you think this old man an eccentric," Zack said, squinting quizzically at Jonathan.

"I am old and wealthy, that allows me certain eccentricities. You might say that inviting you here, in a way, makes you a project of my eccentricity. In any event, whatever the outcome, I immodestly know that this interview is a big career step for you, so you are receiving a value for your time."

Zack was right, Jonathan had benefited from Zack's generosity for years and that generosity extended to the interview. Still, Jonathan didn't know if he should be insulted or flattered.

"Let's get started and help me prove that Marie, Becky, and I have been good judges of character; then, and now," Zack slapped the table with a flat hand, picked up a scone and took a bite.

Chapter Eight

Down to Business

Jonathan scrunched his shoulders up to his ears and shook to loosen up before he spoke.

"Gathering information about your numerous enterprises for this interview was not easy. You are an extraordinary example of entrepreneurial achievements. Readers will want to know how you became so successful. Can you help by giving me some indication of the number of businesses you started, own, or have invested in?"

Zack looked thoughtful and scratched the back of his neck. "Well, I am officially retired from day-to-day business activities. Now I am the chairman of the board of a private family trust, holding company. You probably know more about the legal and accounting structure than I do."

"Are you trying to avoid the question or being humble?"

"Neither, our investments are in a constant state of flux. We sell our interests in some businesses—invest in new, and spin-off others. Our accountants can supply any information that they feel can be shared. I'll alert them to expect a call from you."

"Please tell me about the structure as you know it to be today."

"The Todd Family Trust is a holding company; it owns the stock of all the family-owned businesses as well as the stock of the businesses where we own a controlling interest. As our family has grown, it became possible for us to have a member of the family in management of all of our interests here and abroad."

"I was able to find the businesses you sold because you continued to serve on the board of directors after the purchase. But I am certain there are others that I could not identify," Jonathan pointed out.

"True, the businesses that we have sold through the years to major corporations are public record. There is a Todd family member serving on each board of the companies in which we still hold stock."

"Do you have a formula for your success?" Jonathan asked.

"Our rule is to stay focused in areas that we know and understand. When we venture into someone else's area of business, it is unknown territory. Therefore, it is always with active management partners who know that business. We limit investment to privately held companies where we will be major, controlling stockholders. Having trusted team members on site, who know their business, and have a stake in it minimizes our risk. We stay with those categories that serve our industry, marketing, distribution, warehousing, freight, even vertical market software development." Zack shrugged as if he tasted something bad. "Computerization was tough for me, I am a technophobe."

"And Marie was active through the years," Jonathan hesitated before continuing.

Zack grinned knowingly, "Let's get the unasked question out of the way. I'm sure you are curious after seeing the portrait of Marie.

"Marie was colored. That's what they called black folks then. Marie was born in Africa. Her mother was the daughter of a tribal chief. Her father was Caucasian. He was an administrator for a French-operated girls' school when he and Marie's mother met. They fell in love, married, had Marie and returned to France together. Marie was considered mulatto."

"I didn't know. I couldn't find any photos of the two of you together in the public archives and her race wasn't mentioned in any of the material I found." Jonathan said.

"I'm happy to hear that." Zack said. "Our racial difference was never an issue with my family and friends. It shouldn't have been anyone else's business but we know prejudices are slow to overcome. Unfortunately, Marie's family took years to accept our marriage. From the start, they were against her marrying an American. They said we were infatuated because of our racial differences and we were too young to make such a commitment. Mostly, they didn't want Marie to leave France. Our kids, their grandchildren, were the catalyst that finally brought us all together."

Zack was holding the half-eaten scone. He put it on his plate and sighed. "Let's leave that for later. Suffice it to say that by the time I was successful enough to be of interest to the media, I didn't want the attention, and my success allowed the power to have my wishes respected."

Jonathan stretched. Spreading his arms, he asked, "Where is everybody? This is a very big house and you seem to be all alone here. Frankly, finding you working in the barn surprised me."

Zack stood and stacked dishes and cups. "Oh, I just help out now and then, the heavy work is done by people much younger." He went to the sink.

"My daughter, Claire, lives here with me. She lost her husband a couple of years before Marie died and came to help us. Claire loves this house and the horses, turns out that we are good for each other.

"We have help, some full-time, some part-time, some just during breeding season. Ben is our full-time farm man and all around handyman. Tim is our full-time stable man.

"During the week, we have Sophie our wonderful housekeeper. She is a rare treasure. She keeps the house, grocery shops, and runs errands; we all share the barn chores when needed, and we all work in the gardens in season. I do most of the cooking. Claire manages the farm, checks the horses every morning first thing and medicates when necessary. We don't keep as many horses here now as we used to; so during quiet times, like now, the workload is light."

Zack rinsed dishes in the sink and Jonathan returned the tub of clotted cream to the refrigerator. "Where are all those people today?" Jonathan asked.

"Sophie is off weekends; Claire is Christmas shopping in the city with a local friend. She left early yesterday to beat the storm. This storm is going to be a big one."

Jonathan let out a low moan that attracted Homer's attention.

Zack was still talking. "Ben and Tim mucked stalls and grained before you arrived. They let the Percheron stallion out for a romp. I gave them both the rest of the day off. They have a part-time snow plowing business and needed time to get their equipment ready. I brought the big black in with a whistle just before you got here and gave the gang some hay to chew on until their dinner time."

"That big black horse startled me on the lane when I arrived. I nearly drove into the rock." Jonathan said.

Zack looked over his shoulder at Jonathan, his grin spread wide. "Oh, sorry to hear that, Percy is playful, gentle, and good-natured, he just doesn't realize that his size is intimidating. That, and the fact that his winter coat makes him appear even larger. He is 19 hands tall and 2600 pounds."

"Percy?" Jonathan said in disbelief. "The name sounds anton-ymous, effeminate; it doesn't seem to fit that animal."

"Marie named the foal at his birth, the original old French percer Val is a strong name. One of her favorite poems was Chré-tien de Troyes—Perceval, the Story of the Grail. She read it in French often. Perceval was one of King Arthur's Knights of the Round Table who was given a glimpse of the Holy Grail. The reg-istered name of the horse is King Arthur's Perceval.

"Marie's life was a search for her personal Grail. To her it was a sacred something that is part of our individual spirit. She called it the uniqueness, a special spiritual consciousness."

Recalling the stallion's birth, Zack paused. Memories came flooding back of all the foals he and Marie witnessed through the years. The colt was only a few months old when Marie died. How proud she would be to see the magnificent specimen he has become at maturity. Then he thought about the birth of each of his children. How Marie and he would marvel at the miracle of new life. It was something neither of them ever took for granted.

Zack leaned forward over the sink and hung his head sadly at the memory of lying beside Marie's frail body in the hospital bed, holding her gently as she took her last breath.

Jonathan had turned toward the window to watch the blowing snow. He was thinking again about leaving before the storm got any worse. When Todd's daughter returns, it will prove that the roads are passable.

"When will Claire be back?"

Zack used a napkin to wipe his eyes. "She'll be back Monday night. She and her friend will be spending the weekend in the city. They are staying at our apartment there. Becky plans to fly in for the holidays, they will meet in the city and all drive back together. You and I can take care of the gang in the barn later."

"Monday, today is Friday!" Jonathan was astonished. "Sorry Mr. Todd, but I am returning to New York as soon as we finish here, you better make other arrangements."

"We'll see, and please, call me Zack!"

Jonathan was trying hard to cover his annoyance at the presumption but suspected Todd knew. He returned to the table and clumsily fumbled with his notes. Buying time to regain composure, he asked about Zack's full first name.

"You use the French spelling, Zacharie," Jonathan flavored his pronunciation, "instead of the Anglo, Zachary. Were your parents from France?"

"My parents were French Canadians. They immigrated to Massachusetts to work in the textile mills. I grew up in a small town east of the Connecticut River." The old man returned to his chair, grinning now at more pleasant memories.

Jonathan flipped his chair and straddled it, his notebook and tape recorder on the kitchen table. "You served in the First World War. Were you drafted?"

Zack scuffed his chair sideways and rested his right elbow on the table. "No, I enlisted before Conscription. The Selective Service Act did not start until the middle of 1917, after my seventeenth birthday. At that time draft registration started at age twenty-one."

"What motivated you to enlist in the army?"

Zack made a temple shape of his fingers and thoughtfully brought them to his chin.

"German U-boats were attacking ships and killing Canadians and Americans. That should have been enough reason, but I admit it was also a youthful fantasy. It seemed like an adventure of a teenage boy. There was much talk about the forming of the Lafayette Escadrille and I hoped to become a pilot. Flying was exciting, the airplane was brand new, and it would revolutionize warfare.

Zack assumed an expression of woeful consideration. "Just as well that I didn't become a pilot. They had a short life expectancy in the early days of the war. Many of us believed that the United States could not depend on oceans to protect us. We thought that if we were to keep our homes and loved ones safe we must keep the fight off our shores. For a young man, at that time, a lot of the motivation was patriotism. Perhaps it was the prideful thing for young men to do.

"My parents brought us all up to believe that our most important purpose on this earth was to take care of one another. To my three brothers and two sisters and me that meant that we each had a purpose to fulfill.

"In 1916, a year before the United States actually entered the war, my older brother, Remi, enlisted in the US Coast Guard. He thought that would be his way of protecting our country and our families. He was already seventeen. My pal Sam enlisted in the army at the same time as Remi. For Sam it was definitely a matter of family pride. Sam's grandfather was a hero; he served in the 54th Massachusetts Regiment during the Civil War."

Jonathan scribbled in his note pad. "Then your friend Sam was black, the 54th Massachusetts Regiment was all African

American. I read a lot about them during my first job in the research department at the paper. The paper was doing a piece about black business leaders, for a Black History Month article."

Zack studied Jonathan for a moment with a look of respect. Then he digressed. "I remember how excited Marie was when Negro History Week was first proposed. That was way back."

"1926," Jonathan offered.

"Yes, Marie was thrilled that Black Americans were being given the recognition they deserved. When President Ford expanded it to the entire month of February in 1976, Marie wrote him a letter of appreciation. He wrote back; still have the letter here somewhere."

"It sounds as though Marie was an activist."

Zack peered over his glasses at Jonathan. "Marie was more of an advocate and a facilitator. She had many interests. When anything came to Marie that she considered a worthy cause, she supported it. Of course, she knew first hand what people of color were facing in their daily lives. She did what she could, when she could, offered financial support when the need presented itself."

"Like your P.I.F. Scholarship Trust?" Jonathan questioned remembering the source of his education funding. "Has it focused on minorities in the past? Does it now?"

Zack picked up something in Jonathan's voice or phrasing. He stared at Jonathan trying to read the meaning in his question. "Jonathan, you know that race wasn't a factor in your case. No, both Marie and I believed that qualification should be on merit and need. When Marie was alive, she sat on the granting committee. The screening committee coded each application by number with no reference to sex or race. After the grant, we identified the recipient. Marie enjoyed following their individual progress and often shared that information with me."

Jonathan furrowed his brow, "Applicants are not identified personally but I was specifically, why was I an exception?"

"Of course you are right, but you know something, Jonathan, I was never really sure about that myself, and never asked. You were important to Marie and that was all I needed to know.

As I remember, Becky spent a lot of time with Marie discussing your circumstances during a visit here. It started one Christmas Eve. Becky had graduated from high school in the spring and started college that fall. She stayed with us over the Christmas break.

"Becky told Marie a story that had a powerful impact on both of them. She was impressed with a young man who was a year behind her in high school. She said mutual friends told her that the young man was working hard to maintain his studies while also working full time to help his family. There was family financial pressure due to his sister's illness. From that point on, Marie and Becky seemed to talk about this young man and his family often, on the telephone as well as when they were together."

So, Becky Baron is at the core of this meeting too. Jonathan thought. But why? During school, we never exchanged more than a couple of words of greeting and those occasions were rare.

She was very attractive and at the time, in Jonathan's immature mind, out of reach for an underclassman. He remembered that he had a crush on Becky, but then so did most of the boys in their school. Becky was the connection. The question now was why he had become so important.

Chapter Nine

First World War

Homer nuzzled Zack gently. "That's right, Homer, it's that time."

The dog's entire body quivered with excitement at Zack's comment. Together they went to an exterior French door and Homer bounded out into the snow. Zack unfolded a large bath towel that had been resting on a nearby chair. Less than a minute passed and Zack opened the door to the now frisky Homer. The old dog looked years younger as Zack briskly rubbed the wet snow off. "You stink now," Zack commented to the dog.

Homer didn't appear to be offended. His toenails clicked a constant rhythm on the wood floor in anticipation of the expected reward.

Zack retrieved a box from the cupboard and rattled it. Homer sat dutifully with tail swishing. Zack returned to the table and pantomimed the routine as Homer faced the man and shook his head side to side making his long ears flap. He sat and gently pawed Zack's knee in a begging fashion.

While Homer crunched the biscuit reward, Zack faced Jonathan and asked, "Are you hungry? It is afternoon and we are still in the kitchen."

Putting up his hands defensively, Jonathan groaned, "I'm stuffed."

"Getting back to my pal, Sam, and World War I, that's an important link to the story you want to write," Zack said.

Jonathan checked his recorder and nodded.

"Sam saw heavy combat during the war. The 369th Infantry Regiment was the first all-black US Army combat unit to enter the war. The French needed troops and American soldiers would not fight alongside a Negro in those days, so General Pershing responded to France's request for troops by assigning the 369th. That was one tough bunch, the 369th. The French government awarded the entire regiment the Croix de Guerre," Zack said with obvious admiration.

"Sam told me that one night in a trench, he was head to head, whispering to a white French soldier to rub some dirt on their faces as camouflage. The soldier made a funny noise. A dark hole appeared in the shocked soldier's forehead and blood trickled down his nose. He toppled over on Sam. Sam said their heads were only a few inches apart, but his dark skin had saved his life. It's important that you make note of Sam serving in France. You'll see when I get to that part of the story."

Zack continued. "I was stuck at home until my seventeenth birthday. In fact, I enlisted on my birthday."

"Did you finish high school?" Jonathan asked.

"High school? No. I left school at fourteen. Most of the boys in my generation, from working families, had to. My first job was working on an old Sanford delivery truck; I drove it some and helped with the truck repairs."

Surprised, Jonathan stated, "You were only fourteen years old and you drove a truck without a driver's license?"

Zack tilted his head forward and slid his glasses down his nose. "What are you inferring, Jonathan? I *could* reach the pedals. At that time, only professional chauffeurs needed a driver's license and I was as interested in keeping the truck running as I was driving. Fiddling with mechanical things was fun then, still is.

When I was sixteen, I even went to Syracuse, to the Sanford Truck plant to see if I could get a job there, no luck. My father got me a job at the mill. He told his boss that I could drive a car and a horse, and fix any machine."

The left corner of Zack's mouth drew up in a grin, "The stories about Samuel Colt working for his dad in a textile mill before starting his firearm's business gave my father's boss reason to think all mechanics were inventors like Sam Colt. He hired me."

"Is that where you met your friend Sam, your future business partner?" Jonathan asked.

"No, Sam Brown and I grew up together. He is gone now, you know, passed away in his sleep. Sam was my oldest and dearest friend," Zack's shoulders drooped and he seemed to become smaller in his chair.

"There couldn't have been many black families living in small New England towns then. Was it common for young blacks and whites to become friends?" Jonathan asked.

Zack leaned forward, elbows on the table; he folded and refolded a paper napkin, "I can only speak from personal experience. In general, Sam and his family fit in. That might have been a rare thing for the times, but that is how it was. A few whites in the community may not have been as tolerant as most, but I can't remember any real trouble. Sam had more challenges when he went out into the world."

Zack stood. "It's time for another break, Jonathan. Homer and I have old bladders. Wander around while I let Homer out— Come-on boy this time we will mess up mudroom."

Jonathan referred to his notes, and scribbled a couple of questions for future reference. He stood and walked around the kitchen stopping to take a closer look at the wide slate sink.

Zack came back and started loading the dishwasher, "More coffee, Jonathan?"

"No thank you," Jonathan almost shouted. He hoped his coffee nerves were finally settling down.

Zack responded to Homer's yelp and let him back in the house. The old dog quickly ran into the warmth of the kitchen, fresh snow accumulated on his back. He shook vigorously. Zack followed, mop in hand.

"Homer, you were supposed to stop inside the door. Com'ere old boy."

Zack dried the last of Homer's melted snow from dog and floor, and then busied himself straightening up while Jonathan leaned against the counter, "You started your import business in 1920, after you came back from overseas. You were very young. How did you finance a business startup? It would have required serious capital. Neither your family nor Sam's family were wealthy."

"It was an interesting turn of events. The months after we came home were difficult. I had fallen deeply in love with a woman in France. I was depressed. We lost contact just before the end of the war and neither of us knew how to reach the other. Then La Grippe, the Spanish Flu broke out. It claimed more lives than World War I combat. Over four hundred thousand died in France, and I feared that I lost the love of my life."

"Was America also hit by the flu?"

"It started in America. Many believe our soldiers probably brought it with them to Great Britain and Europe. They called it the grippe here, over six hundred thousand Americans died.

The Spanish Flu sounded familiar to Jonathan but he couldn't remember much about it.

Zack stared at the whiteout beyond the kitchen window. "Losing so many friends and loved ones over such a short period of time, I sank into deep depression. When I came home, I did not want to go back to the mills. Sam and I considered going to Canada where the Canadian government was offering land enticements for young men. But Sam was worried about going anywhere that his race would be an issue. He was talking about going back to France. He thought he was treated better there. The thought of returning to France appealed to me as well, but neither of us could afford it. We became the odd couple and lived in a shack on his father's small farm. We helped Sam's dad some and took odd jobs together for a while.

"Sam kept in touch with a Frenchman he met during the war. The man was Sam's senior non-commissioned officer while Sam's regiment served with the French Army. The two men were the same age and became close friends.

"Sam's friend's name was Jean-Paul, his family had a vineyard in the Bordeaux Region. Before the outbreak of the war, Jean-Paul's father was investigating exporting his wine to America. Jean-Paul's father was killed during the war and his siblings died of the flu. After that, he took over the vineyards and winery operations. He and other family members were again giving exporting serious thought.

"One day, Sam received a letter from Jean-Paul. He asked if Sam could help by recommending someone capable of establishing a distribution of his wine in the US. He asked Sam about his friend. During the war, Sam bragged about his white friend that had the gift of gab. He told him that I was a born salesman and spoke fluent French. What he didn't tell Jean-Paul is that I was as dirt poor as Sam and neither of us had any business connections.

"When Sam got the letter he suggested that the two of us approach Jean-Paul about working together. We knew nothing about wine or importing and we didn't have any money, but we had brass whatchacallits and we didn't know any better.

"Trading companies controlled exports, pooled product, and added high markups. Jean-Paul loved his vineyards and his winery, but hated the business of selling the product. He wanted to find a way around using a trading company. He could ship the product but he needed distribution here in the States. Jean-Paul came to the US. He trusted Sam and liked me. He thought we were ambitious and that with opportunity and direction we would help him make a success of his venture. He convinced his family to set up an American import company of their own and offered Sam and me jobs.

"Being a brash sort of fellow, I suggested that Sam and I should partner with the French in the American company, working on a percentage of sales, pointing out that the arrangement would be more motivating. Surprisingly the French agreed. We offered some potential. Sam's French was bad, but mine was good and Jean-Paul's English was good, so between us, we communicated well. Jean-Paul's family agreed, set up the American company and financed our startup expenses.

"Sam and I went back to France with Jean-Paul where the details were worked out. We worked for a few weeks beside Jean-Paul and his people to get a quick education about the wine business.

"As soon as Sam and I got home we rented a warehouse. It was an exciting time. There were bumps in the road but Jean-Paul came over to help and he was true to his word with necessary financing. We structured our business relationship, retained a reputable law firm and an accounting firm that understood the import business and would keep us out of trouble.

"In the beginning all I did was travel from one prospect to another. I contacted wholesalers and distributors along with private stores and made my pitch. Many didn't take me seriously, some thought they could take advantage of my youth and inexperience, and tried to do just that. When the wine proved to be popular and began to sell, relationships were established."

The kitchen was quiet, with only the low hum of the refrigerator and the sound of the wind blowing snow against the kitchen window. Both men stood, leaning against the counter.

At 1:15 p.m., Jonathan stole a look at his watch. He calculated that the storm would add an hour travel time on his return trip to New York and processed the best way to accelerate the interview. Turning to Zack, he asked, "How did you meet Marie?"

Arms folded, head tilted dreamily at the question, Zack responded, "We met in northern France during the war. Marie and her friend, Yvette, were nurses at a nearby hospital.

"Marie was a couple of years older than I was. The first time I saw her I knew she would be the woman I would marry. Looking at me, the green kid, I think it took Marie longer to come to that conclusion.

"I was a love-sick puppy. Marie would disappear for long periods. There were times that I thought I had lost her. On one occasion, she and some of the other nurses transferred to a field hospital unit. A bomb hit the hospital and the reports said there were no survivors.

"My heart sunk, I broke down in tears. I was desolate. Then, one evening, I was passing the hospital when I heard a group talking together as they approached. My heart jumped. One of the female voices was familiar. She was speaking in English with a heavy French accent."

"Marie was alive. That was Marie?" Jonathan said excitedly.

"It was Yvette. It was blackout conditions. There was some moonlight. I strained to see if Marie was with her. As they came nearer, a familiar figure was part of the group, it was, Marie. The sight of her filled me with the greatest joy I had ever experienced.

"Marie didn't speak, but Yvette told me how she and Marie were not at the hospital when it was hit. They were with a transport unit when the bomb hit the hospital. For several days, they treated wounded survivors from the area of the explosion.

"Marie stood in the shadows like a beautiful apparition without saying a word. I couldn't tell if she saw the relief and the love in my eyes. Later she told me that in the midst of the turmoil after the hospital bombing she kept thinking about me, wondering if she would ever see me again. She was as deeply concerned about my safety and survival as I was about hers."

"So, did Marie come home with you?" Jonathan asked.

"No, the war dragged on, we lost touch. Then the flu hit. So many young people died."

Jonathan watched Zack as the old man gazed sidelong toward a snow-blurred window.

"How much do you know about World War I, Jonathan?"

"Only what little I remember from high school and a few TV documentaries. My mom's grandfather was killed in action."

"Yes, Sam and I were fortunate, we came home alive and in one piece. My brother, Remi, died in the Bristol Channel."

"In England? I thought you said he joined the United States Coast Guard?"

"The US Coast Guard was absorbed into the US Navy during the war. Remi served on board the Tampa, it was a convoy escort. He made over 100 trips through U-boat-infested waters from Gibraltar to Britain. In 1918, the Tampa was escorting a convoy to Wales in the Bristol Channel. The Tampa steamed out ahead, probably as a decoy. The other ships heard a loud explosion. A search found a few pieces of wreckage and two unidentifiable bodies. The Tampa sunk with 130 good men. The folks in Wales appreciated what the American sailors were doing for them. They honored the two Coast Guardsmen with a military burial in a local churchyard.

"One of the bodies was later identified and brought to the states. The other, the unknown sailor, still rests in that churchyard," Zack paused. "You know, the local citizens care for his grave to this day. I make it a point to visit that grave whenever I can. My brother, Remi, may be resting there. Even if it isn't Remi, the young sailor who gave his life deserves my respect."

Despite the passing of decades, Jonathan could see that the old man was still touched with remorse. Jonathan stayed quiet until Zack was ready to speak again. Zack folded a dishtowel, tossed it onto the counter and returned to his chair at the table. Jonathan followed and took a seat.

"When we first landed in France we were excited and scared to death," Zack murmured.

Jonathan was captivated, he studied Zack, this was the first person he met with World War I experience. "When I was in public school we didn't get into war history much. In college, Vietnam was the primary war topic. Many instructors were protestors during the Vietnam era and some had gone to Canada to avoid the draft."

Jonathan continued, "I met a couple of veterans who served over there but they never said much about their Vietnam experiences."

Zack raised an eyebrow. "I am not surprised about veterans not speaking about Vietnam considering the shabby treatment they received when they returned. There were many Americans who thought that the war was a mistake, but I think the world would be very different if it had not occurred, and not for the better."

Zack's face pinched in question, "You say there wasn't much war history study in school. What is happening in our schools?" Zack was visibly upset. "There is a great quote: 'those who cannot remember the past are condemned to repeat it,'" Zack stated. "Didn't you read any of the George Santayana writings, Jonathan, didn't you read Reasons and Common Sense in college?"

Jonathan responded, "I have heard that quote stated differently."

"And inaccurately I suspect!" Zack snapped. "There is another: 'only the dead have seen the end of war.' That's another quote from Santayana, but Plato gets credit for that one," Zack thundered.

Jonathan watched Zack's face as it colored, "Come to think of it, I read somewhere a few years ago that Santayana was often quoted and rarely read. Too bad, good stuff, the five volumes are in my library, take a look."

At the mention of the library, Jonathan again experienced the vision he had earlier at the library doorway. It returned with the same intensity then merged with the earlier vision in the stable. Just as quickly, the room darkened, and a wave of nausea swept over Jonathan. He trembled. He smelled a metallic, coppery odor that made him want to scream at some unseen horror.

Zack's voice came from the distance, "Are you all right boy? Jonathan, what's the matter?" Zack asked with concern.

Awash in perspiration, Jonathan answered weakly, "Just a little indigestion, I stopped in town for breakfast and it doesn't seem to agree with me. Then, I wolfed down two of those great scones."

"Do you need anything, a drink of water?"

Jonathan shook his head negatively and Zack moved to his chair at the table. Jonathan instinctively followed.

"You were talking about World War I, let's continue, I'm feeling better already."

Jonathan was silent as Zack adjusted his body and shrugged his shoulders for comfort. "American soldiers got a fast education from the Brits and the French. They told us that the Black Hand, terrorists, assassinated Archduke Franz Ferdinand of Austria and his wife. That was the trigger. It was like throwing angry dogs together into a pit. Austria invaded Serbia and all hell broke loose. Because of treaties, countries from around the world were involved.

"There is an important lesson from history here. A small radical group turned up the heat that started the pot boiling. We have to be careful today and in the future that such a thing doesn't happen again," Zack stated emphatically.

"Did you see combat?" Jonathan asked.

"I never shot anyone if that's what you want to know. I was a mechanic, a driver, and a stable man. There was plenty of action around me and I had an experience in the trenches but it was brief. War experiences molded my life and I will never forget them. I saw unbelievable horror, extraordinary bravery, and reckless stupidity. I also saw spirituality and great humanitarianism.

"One time when I was driving a supply truck from the depot to the front I was stranded, pinned down for a couple of very long days. I witnessed life in the trenches. They say there are no atheists in foxholes. Believe me, that is a true statement! We all prayed and vowed that if we lived to return home we would make the best life we could for others and ourselves. That experience opened my eyes and heart to other human beings." The uncommon resonance and unique inflection in Zack's voice added substance to his comments.

"It gave me some personal insight too. I learned to trust instinct, seize opportunity, draw upon experience, and finish what I started. I have been able to stick to those principles. It was not always easy, and I did not always reach the goal I set, or realize the outcome I wanted. But for the most part I have very few regrets." Zack showed some discomfort. "Enough of the war, let's move on."

Chapter Ten

Midge is Concerned

1:05 p.m.

Midge stood in the restaurant kitchen, business was slow due to the storm. "Do you think we should close early," she asked. "We haven't had a customer for over an hour. My bones were right earlier, now they are screaming. This is going to be a big storm; I want to get home safely."

The mild-mannered Jake flashed his trademark grin under his reversed ball cap. "Babe, I've always loved your bones and I'd be happy to take them home early. But, are you sure that you are not picking up something else on your notorious radar?"

"Well, you know the young man that came in earlier; the one I told you about from New York? He came in with company. You know what I mean, 'that' kind of company! Don't get me wrong, it was good, loving company. But he also had a beautiful aura, the kind that makes me feel he is a very old soul."

Jake interrupted, smiling lovingly. "Edgar Casey had nothing on you. Are you telling me you think this New Yorker is a reincarnation of someone special?"

"It could be he is one of the star-crossed lovers who jumped from Redemption Ridge." Midge offered.

"Or, he could be one of the murderous spurned lovers, the 'if we can't live together, we'll die together' twisted jumpers. Or, maybe he is Oakwood, the guy that killed his wife and her lover at the farm a century ago."

Midge frowned thoughtfully. "Yes, the timing could be right. I've read a lot about reincarnation. When some people are regressed to prior lives, they describe a resting period. They usually do not come back right away. Sometimes the resting period is one hundred, even two hundred years."

Jake's eyes twinkled, "Do you think we might have been star-crossed lovers a hundred years ago, come back together now?" he asked jokingly.

"Don't knock what you don't know, wise guy. It could be."

Jake looked at Midge, he removed his hat and held it over his heart. "I wish I could believe that you and I will keep coming back together, over and over." He tossed his hat away, grabbed Midge and kissed her playfully.

"Stop that, this is serious."

"So am I," Jake said grinning lecherously and wiggling his thick eyebrows in a Groucho Marx impression.

"Well, while I was talking to this Jonathan fellow, he told me he was going to the Todd place and wanted to confirm directions. My heart skipped and my tummy danced."

"Okay, but what if he is as you think, returning to the scene. What can be accomplished? Why do you think he is here?"

"It's Redemption Ridge. Maybe he is being drawn to find the love of his life that he was separated from by death."

"Yeah, or maybe he was drawn here to be punished for talking some innocent young woman into jumping off a ledge with him 150 years ago. On the other hand, maybe this guy, in another life, lured a woman to the cliff after she dumped him so he could kill her. He pushed the girl, she hung on to him, and he fell with her accidentally. Did you ever think that some of those lover's leap stories might not have been so romantic after all? Maybe the object of a man's affection might not have wanted to die, just because daddy didn't like the boyfriend, or because she was married to someone else. Maybe the upset affair was only a fling."

"All that is possible, Jake, but this time what I felt was deep sorrow," Midge said with concern. "He had a lot of entities around him—so many it was hard for me to concentrate on him."

"Hey Babe, you can't take on the world's problems, ya know. I just wish some of that extra company people have with them were paying customers," Jake joked.

"Really Jake, I'm concerned. While I was talking to him, I saw the young man's car skidding on ice. Do you think we could ride up Ridge Lane on the way home to be sure everything is all right at the Todd place?"

"Sure Babe, I'll do anything for you."

Chapter Eleven

Searching for Marie

The storm began to intensify. Howling wind gusts shook the French doors and ice crystals chattered against the panes. Jonathan stood and slowly paced around the kitchen. New fears welled up. He stopped and stared at Zack, "Are we safe here, this house is old, what happens if we lose power?"

Zack tipped back his chair, "You are the anxious one, aren't you? Relax; this house has stood through many storms. If the utility company's overhead lines break, our generators kick in automatically. The terminal house down at the lane serves all the farm buildings with underground cables."

"Let's get back to business Jonathan, it will take your mind off the weather."

Jonathan glanced back at the flexing doors, and then sat across from Zack at the table. He searched for a way to cover his embarrassment. Clearing his throat, he said, "I'm still curious about how you and Marie finally got together. Are you stringing out the story on purpose?"

"Marie didn't enter the picture for a while. Sam and I put in long hours and the hard work paid off. Jean-Paul expanded the wine export side with varieties from other regions of France. By 1922, we had assembled profitable networks on both the export and import sides of the businesses. We were doing well enough to consider adding other products. Sam and I went back to France together. He spent time with Jean-Paul visiting the vineyards while I scouted for new product possibilities."

"And searched for Marie, I'll bet," Jonathan interjected impatiently.

Beaming from the thought, Zack continued, "Time had not cooled my love for her. Marie was always on my mind. We knew so little about each other. I didn't know where to start looking for her. Then there was the nagging worry that she might not have survived the war or the flu.

"One morning before the end of the war, I woke to find Marie and Yvette gone, transferred overnight. I tried to find her before leaving France, without success. We never spent any private time together or shared personal information. I thought I had lost her.

"However, despite my fears, I didn't give up. I wanted to believe that Marie was alive and we would meet again. My fantasy was for us to meet on the street, Marie would see me and run into my arms," Zack stated through a wide grin.

Jonathan interrupted excitedly. He approached Zack and gestured theatrically, "Let me guess, you met Marie again when you visited Paris. You walked into a coffee shop on Avenue des Champs-Elysées and she sat alone at a back table obviously in despair, waiting for you! I could write a book about it," Jonathan said with flourish.

"Close, but not quite," Zack said enjoying their interplay.

"It was in a small, dirty, little French town. I walked down a narrow alley and entered a dismal perfume laboratory to see if the lab's product had export potential—"

Jonathan interrupted, "And there she was!"

"No, Marie was sitting at a sidewalk café in the town square. My smell drew her attention; the perfume factory odor still clung to my clothing.

She recognized me and called to me in French, with her exaggerated pronunciation of my name, 'Zack-Kair-ee.' It was the sweetest sound I could have heard," Zack was beaming.

"L'Amour triompe de tout," Jonathan said. "Love conquers all."

Zack grinned appreciatively, "Something like that; and you should brush up on your French pronunciation."

Zack continued, "You cannot imagine how excited each of us was. Bursting with joy would be an understatement. We both knew we were meant for each other—to be together. We were married before leaving France. It could have been a happier ceremony if Marie's parents had attended, but we made the best of it. Marie and I had been through very difficult times. Between the war, separation, and the flu epidemic each of us lived with the fear we had lost the love of our lives forever. Then fate stepped in."

"How did you know you and Marie were compatible? It could have been infatuation. From what you tell me, you and Marie were not intimate before you married. You never kissed before your reunion."

Zack studied Jonathan. "I know that times have changed. In my day, it was rare for two people of the opposite sex to live together as lovers without being married. A moral man would not put the woman he loved in such a position where she might later have been disgraced. Being old school, I am not objective on this subject."

Jonathan asked, "Did Sam participate in the marriage ceremony?"

"Sam and Marie's friend Yvette were our witnesses. We married in a small Catholic church. Without her parents in attendance, it was painful for Marie. They would not attend the ceremony and did not come to the ship to see us off. We came to the States as husband and wife. A year later our first son was born.

"Let's move along." Zack waved Jonathan off the subject and said, "I'm sure we will get to the substance of what you are looking for. It seems we are digressing too much. Don't you have a list of questions? The standard stuff, you know, it seems that every article I read about a person is formularized."

Jonathan grinned, "I did put together a list of questions, and yes, they are the standard formula. However, that was when I expected to be interviewing a grumpy invalid, secured in a drafty mansion, surrounded by servants. After meeting you and being here in your home, I decided that this story is going to be different. I don't work for the paper anymore, so I have the freedom to give this piece personality. Marie played an important role in your life and in your business."

The corners of Zack's eyes wrinkled, his mustache twitched, and the hint of appreciation turned up the corners of his mouth.

"That's true. Marie was a wonderful mother and a supportive partner. She raised our four children and helped Sam and me in our business. She was a great asset; dealing with our French partners. Her French was perfect and she had good business sense."

"So you, Sam, and Marie were born-entrepreneurs," Jonathan stated.

"Hardly, we learned by trial and error. Looking back, knowing what I know, I probably would not have taken the risk that the French took with a couple of inexperienced kids. We survived and prospered in some ways in spite of ourselves. Fortunately we were respected veterans, importing popular products during an economic boom, after the war."

"When your story is published, I think the readers would like to know what management lessons you learned, building the early business, that helped you expand and start subsequent businesses."

Zack thought a minute. "There were so many it's difficult to know where to begin, but I think putting the right people in the proper place would be among the most important.

"Sam and I divided responsibilities and duties. In the beginning, before Marie joined us, I was responsible for sales, distributor relations, and the communications with France because of language issues. My French was better than Sam's was.

"Sam was better with detail. He was a whiz at keeping the books, tracking orders and better at product distribution, detail, and shipping. When Marie joined us, she became our direct link to France, processing orders. I expanded our sales efforts. That was my forte. When the time came to hire new people the three of us conferred. It did not take long to realize that there was no formula for hiring good people. A good personality wasn't a substitute for ambition, a superior education wasn't a substitute for good common sense, and experience in a related field didn't always transfer well to our business."

"Can you be specific? How did it relate to your workers, your human resources?"

Zack recoiled, "Human resources, ha! I remember the first time I heard the term it was unfamiliar. You college folks have fancy titles and definitions for everything. Our employees were our people, like family, not resources. Oh, and by the way, we did not call employees 'workers' then, that was a term used by communist party leaders to describe lower class subjects.

"Marie, Sam, and I were good together. We recognized the difference in values between education, experience, drive, aptitude, and good judgment. We would hire a college graduate for a warehouse job with the thought of promoting him or her into management after they proved themselves and learned the business. We advanced from within but only when certain that we were not promoting a good person to a position beyond their ability to grow.

"To an MBA like you, this must seem elementary, but I have witnessed corporate politics. It is easy for an unqualified person to slide up the corporate ladder if they play the game." Zack acted disgusted, "What's it called?"

"It's called Peter's Principle." Jonathan commented.

Zack explained that through the 1920s the import business thrived. He, Marie, and their partners were all optimistic about the future.

"Okay, you said that the twenties were boom times, certainly not the late twenties." Jonathan questioned.

"True, in October of 1929 the economic future was bleak. Sam came to me, depressed. He had invested heavily in the stock market and needed money. His children were young and he wanted to spend more time with them. Jean-Paul was in poor health and his family wanted to sell their share of our import company to Marie and me, conditional upon a long-term contract to continue importing their wines.

"Marie and I were careful with our money. We had not invested in the stock market. Instead, we invested, privately, in a number of small businesses that were doing well in spite of the Depression. In any event, we didn't think the Depression would last long, so we bought out both our American and European partners and attempted to expand the company's product lines. There were obstacles, but in time, we imported a wide diversity of products from Europe and the United Kingdom and other continents."

Zack stood and went to start the dishwasher. He waved off Jonathan's feeble attempt to assist.

The storm chattering on the glass caught Jonathan's attention again. When Homer went out earlier, the snow was below the step, now it piled above the base of the door.

"I really should be going."

Zack turned, his expressions telling. "I think that you know that isn't a good idea. Why don't you go into the library and make yourself comfortable. If you want, you can stoke the fire. I'll clean up here, and then I'll join you."

Chapter Twelve

Midge and Jake on the Lane

S torm-clad, Midge and Jake huddled inside the cab of the pickup as it rolled down Ridge Lane. The wipers throbbed to keep the windshield clear and wind shook the four-wheel drive truck.

"Babe, I thought you told me that you never want to go near the ridge. Can't imagine how important this New York fellow must be if you want to be here in a blizzard," Jake said.

"I don't like it one bit and you know why. Thank you for reminding me. A couple of generations back, a cousin and his sweetheart jumped to their deaths from the peak. We might be driving over the very spot where they died. My family repeats that story over and over. When I was young it kept me awake nights," Midge shifted nervously in her seat, "just get close enough to see the house."

Jake turned into the driveway; there were no fresh tracks ahead. He drove slowly to within a storm-shrouded view of the warmly lit house. A car parked near the front door wore a white covering. Smoke flowed from one of the farmhouse's chimneys.

"Everything looks okay to me, Babe. What do you say that we go home now?" Jake said.

"Yes, I feel better. Thanks sweetheart," Midge said with feeling, as she snuggled against her man. "Wish I could be sure that everything will turn out okay. Do you think I'm crazy, worrying about someone I hardly know?"

"Hey, you are a sweet, caring, and sexy woman. I wouldn't want you to be any different."

"I asked you if you think I'm crazy," Midge goaded Jake.

"Not crazy, just a little strange sometimes, but in a good way," Jake teased. "As far as the weird stuff is concerned, that's okay too. I don't know where it comes from but I don't question it." Jake chuckled. "Too bad it doesn't work for predicting lottery numbers." He turned the big truck around and headed for home.

Chapter Thirteen

In the Library

Passing the large picture window, Jonathan peered out at the blowing snow. A dim image of his reflection peered back.

At the library doorway, Jonathan became aware of the indefinable fragrance and with stark reality found himself standing in the white gazebo. Like the vision in the barn, it was another warm, summer day; vines, heavy with fragrant blossoms entwined the structure. A bee buzzed by. The mysterious woman standing with him gazed into the distance. Narrow beams of light penetrated the lattice and played on her flaxen hair. She turned slowly, gazing lovingly into Jonathan's eyes. Those beautiful eyes, Jonathan thought. The vision was exciting yet painful.

The sound of broken logs dropping in the nearby fireplace brought Jonathan back and he moved into the library. The room was gloomy from the darkness of the stormy day. Smoking embers still glowed in the hearth and the pungent odor of burning wood filled the room.

Jonathan found what he needed in a large brass bucket in the corner of the room. The embers were hot enough to ignite the dry kindling and soon the split logs he added burned brightly. He sank into the deep soft chair to the right of the fireplace and watched the dancing flames taste the new wood.

Suddenly the flames died. Everything went black. Jonathan's mind wrenched to regain reality. The darkness gave way to shadows, blurred sounds, and the odor of death. Straining to see, he recognized the shape of a twisted body covered with dark wet splotches. There was something else, a heavy pressure squeezed his chest and he gasped for breath. Another shape appeared. Someone was standing over him.

"Nice fire," Zack commented as he entered the room and sat in his favorite chair. Homer lazily followed. The dog curled up, butt-end to the hearth.

Jonathan heard Zack's voice, an echo in the distance. He wanted to waken from the horrifying nightmare. He struggled to reunite his mind with his body. His thoughts swirled. What is happening to me? Am I ill? Have I been drugged?

Slowly Jonathan began to understand what Zack had said. With concentrated effort, he muttered, "Boy Scout training."

The last hallucination upset him so much Jonathan's recovery took several moments. Shaking off the shock of this apparition was far more difficult than the other episodes. He stood and stretched, hoping he had not betrayed his emotional distraction. He kept his head turned away from Zack, opened the fireplace glass and stabbed at the logs with a poker. It appeared that Zack had not noticed his behavior. He stretched again and took a position standing behind his chair, facing Zack.

Zack blew out a fresh pipe and filled it expertly. He tested the draw and then he struck a wooden match. When the sulfur had burned off, he passed the match over the surface of the bowl, took a couple of puffs and settled back. *The boy is daydreaming, again, strange young man, at times, Jonathan seems to have trouble focusing.*

Jonathan watched Zack intently. After the false light, Zack tamped the tobacco with a tool, then swirled another flaming match over the bowl. He puffed slowly and appreciatively. Watching the old man's ritual was mesmerizing.

Zack picked up the conversation where they had left off in the kitchen, "It wasn't easy operating in the 1930s, recovery from the Great Depression was slow."

Jonathan snapped back, returned to his chair, and turned on the small tape recorder.

"You can imagine transportation and communications were not what they are today. Marie and I were running the business alone. We didn't have Sam's assistance or Jean-Paul's family money anymore. However, Jean-Paul's family business had expanded; they were exporting wines and other products to other countries and we continued to enjoy a close working relationship. They assisted us in directly importing other products, avoiding intermediaries.

"Most important, we had each other. Marie was the best partner a man could ask for. Together we were an unbeatable team. Moving ahead after the Depression and before the Second World War was very difficult. Our capital was stretched due to the buyout. There were many anxious moments."

"You don't appear to have the personality of a hard-driven businessman. Building any business during wartime and the Depression must have been extremely difficult. It's hard for me to imagine you as a tough negotiator. You said that Sam was the financial guy; was he also the tough member of the partnership?"

"You want to know what I was like when I was younger, Jonathan? Are you hoping to get quotes from me saying something derogatory about myself so you can put them into a book?"

Whoa. That hit too close to home. Jonathan was just thinking that it would not be difficult to fill three hundred or more pages with the Zackarie Todd story, and juicy self-deprecation quotes help to sell books.

Jonathan could feel the warm color entering his face again, he squirmed and tried to lie by ignoring the spot Todd put him in. "It will help me to accurately represent you and the reasons for your success in my article," Jonathan said a bit sheepishly.

Zack gave Jonathan his most penetrating stare. He drew on his pipe, extending the delay in the conversation.

If he backed off too far there was a good chance that this interview could end as well as the chance to write the story. Jonathan replayed the past few minutes in his mind before he spoke.

"It would help to have a personal evaluation of your early business life portrayed. You seem to be the proverbial straight arrow. I have learned enough about entrepreneurial efforts from my time with the paper to realize that there are moral and ethical challenges. All I need is a snippet of how you dealt with necessary compromises. This will add credibility. Perhaps we can discuss your thoughts, off-the-record. We can decide together what will be used."

Jonathan could tell by the look on his face that Zack was not buying this baloney. Nevertheless, something in the old man's expression hinted that he was considering the possibility.

"No," Zack said confidently, "not off the record. Marie brought us together for a reason. I have decided to trust you. You won't betray my trust, will you, Jonathan?"

Squirming again, Jonathan said, "I'll let you see my draft before anything is published."

"Will you write anything that isn't true?"

"Of course not."

"I have your word that everything you write about our meeting will be true."

"Yes."

"Then that will do."

Both men relaxed with their intellectual fencing over. "I'll let you decide what to print. I admit that I bent the rules in order to succeed."

"That's hard to imagine."

"I started building a business during a rough and tough time. The competition didn't play by any set of rules. I had to do what was necessary."

"Can you give me an example?"

"I bribed influential people and delivered wine and beer during Prohibition; those alone were major crimes."

"How could you do that? You described Marie as saintly. I'm sure she would not have allowed you to be dishonest or disreputable."

"Dishonest, disreputable—Jonathan, I wouldn't go that far. Don't forget, I was a young buck then. To me, there was some justification in doing what was necessary to succeed, having put my life on the line for my country. I had responsibilities, employees, contractual commitments, and obligations.

"As for Marie, she did the books after we bought Sam out, and she knew about most of it. Marie and I thought Prohibition was a farce. We had contracts with the European wineries and breweries that, if nothing else, were a matter of personal honor."

"Do you feel the war affected your ethics, your principles?"

"You could say that. It was a slow development of pragmatism. At the time, perhaps my ethics and principles were not really developed. My life was sheltered up to then. Processing the experiences of the war took time. Some lessons were immediate. I watched men kill other men in battle with the same coldness of killing a rat in the trenches. The same men cried for a wounded or killed comrade.

"Our soldiers would search the dead on the battlefield for boots because their feet were swollen so badly from trench foot they could no longer wear their own. Going back and forth to the front with supplies, I saw things I wish I could forget. At first, I was appalled at the inhumanity of it all; in time, I understood the rationality.

"The first time I saw a soldier sitting on the ground unwrapping and re-wrapping his diseased feet, I wretched. You could see the pain etched in his face as he tugged on a dead German soldier's boots. He heard me and saw my reaction. I remember his exact words; 'He ain't got any use for them now, kid,' he was right. The poor dead German didn't need his boots anymore."

Both men were quiet for several minutes. The clock in the foyer ticked loudly then struck the hour. Jonathan cleared his throat and said, "You paid bribes. How did you justify that?"

"I saw it as a necessary overhead to keep a business alive that supported hundreds of good families."

"Selling alcohol when it was against the law during Prohibition, that's what the mob did. That was definitely breaking the law. Were you a rumrunner or a bootlegger?" Jonathan asked.

The left corner of Zack's mouth flicked in amusement, "Jonathan, you have an inaccurate perception of Prohibition. People never stopped drinking. I was neither, I was an importer. At the time, adjustments needed to be made as to how we imported the wine and beer that I distributed. It required creative thinking."

Jonathan interrupted. "I don't think I ever paid much attention to how Prohibition started, or why it ended."

Zack lazily tapped his pipe in a large ashtray. He took a cleaner from the stand and ran it through the stem. "Before Prohibition, employers were complaining about employee drunkenness on the job; mothers complained that the old man bought booze instead of milk for the baby, and after the war, the fact that beer was imported from an enemy, Germany, many supported the case for curbing intoxicating drink.

"The temperance movement was for moderation and restricting alcoholic beverage to low-content beer and wine but when the 18th Amendment passed, it prohibited all intoxicating beverage sales in the United States. Then the Volsted Act needed to be passed to give the government the teeth to enforce the law."

Zack shook his head. "But Americans didn't give up drinking, and mobsters got rich on illegal and sometimes poisonous booze. During the 1920s, speakeasies grew as a cottage industry and gangsters were shooting one another in the streets. Nobody much cared and it didn't seem that anyone was interested in putting an end to Prohibition. Americans kept drinking.

"My biggest problem was not fear of being caught by the government; it was fear of the mob. I kept a very low profile and my customers protected me as a valuable resource. Don't forget, I was providing quality products so I could afford to be careful in my choices of distribution. My customers were the customers I had before Prohibition."

"Like most things the government sticks its nose in, Prohibition was all politics, it started in order to get votes and ended to get tax dollars. Prohibition was supposed to have been evidence of concerned politicians getting involved in a moral, as well as a social issue. They attacked the evil drink with some justification.

However, the side effect was reduced alcohol tax revenue. The reduced tax revenue wasn't immediately obvious though, because in 1913, the 16th Amendment was passed, that instituted the personal income tax.

"Money was pouring in. The 1920s were very prosperous and America was celebrating after World War I. At first, the politicians hardly noticed the lost revenue that the government once received from liquor sales taxes and alcoholic beverage import duties. Then the Depression reduced income tax revenue and the government felt the pinch. Politicians started looking for new income sources. What they found was an old one that could be reinstated—tax on liquor sales and alcoholic beverage import duties.

"However, there was a problem that needed to be addressed. To recover the tax income and import duties on alcohol meant the necessary repeal of 16th Amendment and Prohibition. The rest is history."

Zack shook his head slowly in disgust. "To my knowledge, the 16th Amendment is the only Constitutional Amendment to ever be repealed. That says something about politicians, doesn't it? The government's moral and social good deed got in the way of tax revenue—so much for politicians taking the moral high ground."

Stunned, Jonathan said, "It sounds as though you were willing to challenge authority and the law if necessary to succeed."

Neither man spoke. Jonathan was processing Zack's words and Zack was contemplative. Both men were oblivious to the crackling of the fire as it mixed staccato with the ticking of the big clock outside the library door.

Jonathan's last and most terrifyingly dark vision began to form again. He was saved from the ghastly scene when Zack cleared his throat and moved to get Jonathan's attention.

"My moral character was compromised during the war. I broke the ultimate law of God and man by contributing to the killing of another human being. I never actually shot an enemy soldier, but I transported the ammunition; the explosives that killed and maimed countless enemy soldiers, and in my book, that was just as bad. Every day on the battlefield, I prayed. I prayed for my own protection and the protection of those in battle. I prayed for the souls of those killed in battle, and for the families that would mourn them. I still pray for their souls and ask forgiveness for mine. Even at my age, I have not been able to comprehend man's inhumanity to one another.

"During the war, I heard officers who were taking credit for a successful engagement with the enemy. They referred to the sacrificed lives of their soldiers as *collateral damage, acceptable losses*. Acceptable, who can objectively make that discernment? What qualifies one person to decide that another person's loss of life is acceptable? Throughout my life, I've heard some say that we should practice the 'Golden Rule' and never harm another. Others say that injuring or destroying another human being is justified to save ourselves, or, if it is for the common good. What is the common good that allows one man to injure or destroy another? The same people that materially harm another will turn around and say we should not do anything to hurt another's feelings. It is all right to destroy a person's life or property, but don't insult them, don't hurt their feelings. Really, does that make any sense at all?" Zack's face flushed again twisted with incomprehension.

"I'm not proud of the fact that I justified any wrong doing in business, but compared to war; well, there is no comparison." Zack's voice trailed off.

As though he was talking to himself, Zack continued. "Since the war, I have lived within Judeo-Christian ethics; I will not do anything that harms man or beast. I pay my fair share of taxes. I obey traffic laws because to do otherwise would be arrogant and dangerous."

Jonathan saw the pain in Zack's face when he spoke of death. He felt a pang of guilt and said, "I apologize, I didn't mean to upset you."

"You said you wanted some personal insight."

Touché, and another point for Zack. Nevertheless, Jonathan decided this would be a good time to change direction.

Chapter Fourteen

Zack's Take on Technology

The fire crackled and the grandfather clock struck the hour.

"You have seen so many technological changes during your life. What has impressed you the most?" Jonathan asked.

Zack stared at the steady flames. "I grew up in a house with a coal stove for cooking and heat, and an ice box for refrigeration. Our toilet was a hole in the ground in the back yard with a telephone booth sized box over it. If you didn't have a horse, you walked.

"Technological development has changed the world I knew for most of my life. It certainly has improved our lives but we have paid a price. Technology should have come with a handbook explaining how to and how not to use it." Zack said.

"I'm not sure that I understand." Jonathan said.

"Technology has provided wonderful tools, but I think it also created and compounded problems of personal development. Each new machine brought to market puts some good folks out of work. Take China for example, with a large population and labor force the country has been slow to mechanize. We say they are backward. Perhaps they have good reason. Do you know how many farm laborers a tractor would put out of work in China?

"When I was growing up everyone was self-reliant. We have become so dependent on a machine to do the labor that when it breaks, most people don't know how to repair the machine, or how to do the machine's job manually. When a machine breaks down, the operator sits and waits for someone else to come along and fix it. We have more people sitting and too few fixing."

"What about television? How did people your age react to the development of television?" Jonathan asked. "I have been told that TV seemed like a science fiction concept when it first was developed."

Zack laughed. "When I was growing up, electricity and the telephone were frightening enough. Some thought they gave off rays that would harm or kill us. Television was certainly miraculous. At first, the concept of television excited Marie and me. We went to a New York television studio to watch a kinescoping of a live play. They set up a motion picture camera and photographed the action from a TV screen so they could broadcast the play again later. It was an honest copy of what happened, mistakes and all.

"TV became the source of entertainment and news in the home as more people had their own set. But TV took attention away from family interaction and social connections. Before television came along, up until the mid-50s, families spent time with each other. We played games together in the evening. We went to movie theaters with our friends and family for entertainment.

"The movie theater was the only place to see film of news events. I remember the rooster crowing at the beginning of the *Warner Pathe News*. Before TV, we listened to radio programs. They exercised our imagination." Zack leaned forward, elbow on his knees.

"I enjoyed *The Green Hornet*, *The Fat Man* and *Gang Busters*. My kids were *Jack Armstrong*, *Sky King*, and *Terry and the Pirates* fans.

Sunday nights we gathered around the console radio to hear Lowell Thomas and Walter Winchell.

"In the early days, television news had straightforward delivery, like radio. We had the *Camel News Caravan* with John Cameron Swayze, solid news anchors like John Chancellor and Edward R. Murrow. News film was like the theater newsreels, honest, unadulterated—at least, I like to think so. Video tape recording and editing came along. In a few years, television had become more like Hollywood, like the motion picture industry, creative deception, and fantasy.

"This is 1990; we are supposed to be enlightened, sophisticated, and able to handle aspects of reality as determined by TV censorship. The censorship is in decline at the same rate as morality. Who knows what they will show on the news in another ten years? And news is the serious side of what the tube presents. I cannot imagine what will be called entertainment."

"It sounds like you are not a fan of television." Jonathan said.

"What I am not a fan of is misuse and abuse. Our intelligence and creativity, ingenuity are gifts. Improved communications, medicine, transportation, safety, and creature comfort have been marvels that I witnessed during my lifetime.

"When I was young I thought vaudeville was wonderfully entertaining. Then it was silent movies, and then came the talkies and going to the movie theater became astounding.

"Television—I bought a television the first time I saw one in a store. When we got it home, we tried to watch the snowy picture whenever we could. Marie would laugh hysterically when I stood on a chair manipulating a rabbit-ears antenna for a better picture." Zack broke into a wide grin and imitated manipulation of an imaginary antenna above his head.

"It was a treat for my kids to be allowed to watch television then. Hollywood has taken over television. They attempt to sculpture our thinking. They minimize immorality and aggrandize violence.

"From what I understand from my grandchildren, who are now raising my great grandchildren, TVs have become substitute nannies, and educators. Parents use television to keep the kids entertained; the tube has become a babysitter. Shows aimed at children distort reality and pander to the kids. TV personalities tell parents how to parent, and preschoolers are told that they are great just being themselves. That may be psychologically healthy in some respects, but the message stops short of encouraging youngsters to reach for a goal, and deal with discouragement.

"I listened for years to my kids talk about raising their kids. Now it is my grandchildren talking about raising *their* kids. Seems to me the message to preschoolers for decades has been that it is not necessary to succeed, only to demonstrate an attempt. The bar is set too low and parents pander. The kids get into school and the real world. Tests measure their accomplishment, not their efforts. Cold reality hits them and the kids become traumatized. But that's okay, because the system employs professionals to treat confused kids, then it tries to overcorrect. By the time young people get to high school the system has given up screwing up the poor kids and the cycle of patting the child on the head and pushing them out the door starts over," Zack observed. "My guess is that few college freshmen are prepared for their next dose of reality and after graduation they face another shock."

"You may be right in general, but most kids become intellectually equipped to deal with the contradictions—I don't think they all become neurotic." Jonathan said.

"I hope you are right, but that doesn't excuse the development of the drug culture. It expanded quickly when comedians on TV, and movie idols joked about getting stoned it was broadcast to millions of young people. College students' use of alcohol was bad enough before dangerous drugs hit the scene."

Jonathan relented to that fact that this could be debated for hours and wanted to move on. He commented, "I saw a closed-circuit TV monitor in the kitchen but I haven't seen a television anywhere else. Where do you get current national and international news?" Jonathan asked.

"There are no televisions here on the first floor; only in the guest bedrooms and in my daughter's room. I listen to the radio for music, local news, and weather. I get the *Berkshire Eagle*, the *Springfield* papers, the *Wall Street Journal* and *New York Times*. I also receive a few foreign newspapers by mail. My daughter alerts me to happenings from her sources; I keep a fax in my room and use it regularly to communicate with friends in many different countries."

Zack stood and turned on more lamps as he continued, "I have serious concerns about how news is presented today in all the media. The level of any disaster has to be astronomical to get our attention. Mass media have taken it on itself to educate the public, form opinion, and set moral guidelines. Distort moral parameters are more like it. Journalists are supposed to be objective, unbiased. The journalist I met during the First World War practiced a simple code of ethics; 'Find the truth and report it.' Today I don't know whom to believe. It seems that many news reporters have an agenda; their political and business interests cause them to bend or ignore the truth. Moral compromise is justified."

Jonathan didn't speak. Personally, he agreed that reporting from some media sources did appear biased, but he did not think it to be as pervasive as Zack thought. In any event, Zack's perspective is what mattered.

When Zack returned to his chair, he peered over his glasses at Jonathan. "As for technology, the fax machine was a real breakthrough. We began by using Western Union's service in the mid-1930s. The ability to send actual photographic copies over a wire sped up order processing and other activities. Western Union's Telefax sent telegrams, documents, proposals, contracts, line drawings, maps, and advertising proofs.

"It was the telefax machine that made it possible for Marie and me to work from here when we made this our permanent home and satellite office. We installed our own machines in the office we attached to the barn. It allowed us to be here more. Our staff in the New York office kept direct communication with us by fax. Telefaxing, being able to send documents was a major improvement. Even today, you would be amazed at how much international news I receive. My old friends around the world clip a news article or write me a note and in minutes, I have it in front of me."

"Zack, the world is coming online, what about electronic mail? It is less costly than fax. Within the next few years, every news media outlet will be available on your home computer screen. You must rely on computers in your businesses."

"We started using computers years ago, don't like them. They are temperamental and expensive. We built special rooms in our warehouse in New York to keep them cool, and employed programmers that spoke their language. The early computers burned more electricity than a small town. But I've lost touch over the years, I'm told they improved.

"There is a terminal and printer in the armoire in Marie's study. Claire uses it. She passes on sales and investment reports. Sometimes someone sends me one of those emails. I don't type, so I answer with a fax. Claire has a small computer on her desk in her bedroom. It has a funny name."

"Mac," Jonathan volunteered.

"What?"

"The name of the computer, is it a Macintosh?"

"Sounds right, it's a funny looking little thing."

Zack continues, "We have a special telephone line for each machine. Give me my fax any day. I can write a note, push a button, and the machine will do the rest. The fax answers the phone itself, all the maintenance it requires is putting in a roll of paper when it needs it."

Zack filled his pipe and picked up his book. Signs that he wanted to take a break.

Chapter Fifteen

What is that Fragrance?

Storm or not, Jonathan thought, I have to get back on the road. I'll have to reschedule with Todd to complete the interview another time. He wrestled with how to approach this with the old man.

In a strange way, Jonathan was saddened at the thought of leaving this place, and Zack.

"Funny, you know, Zack, I feel like I have been here before. This room, these windows, they seem so familiar."

No response, his pipe rested in an ashtray, the book lay open in his lap. Zack was asleep.

Jonathan realized that he had not gone to the john for hours. When he stood, it woke Zack. Jonathan gestured toward the bathroom he used earlier in the rear of the house.

"Might as well use the bathroom closest to the guest room, upstairs," Zack said and directed Jonathan to the stairs.

"There should be a new razor and toothbrush, towels—anything you'll need. I'll get some of my grandson's work clothes for you for when we do the barn chores, and you can wash your city clothes tonight."

Again with the, "You're-stuck-here-friend," Jonathan thought, but he didn't comment.

It was still mid afternoon, but the day darkened steadily. Jonathan switched on a lamp in the entry hall and grinned at the elongated shadow he threw. He felt elated, the familiarity of the surroundings mixed with a bittersweet melancholy. Over the smell of the fire and Zack's pipe, he detected a sweet fragrance. Was it perfume? No, some kind of flower, Jonathan never could tell the difference, but it was pleasant and seemed to be eliciting another memory.

Jonathan climbed the stairs to the murky hall above. At the top, he searched for a light switch. A timer clicked as though on queue and a small lamp brightened on an antique credenza. Jonathan turned to view the balcony that circled the stairwell. The familiarity of what he could see in the dim light was astonishing. He racked his brain; perhaps he saw photos somewhere of a similar balcony.

The credenza held numerous photographs. Jonathan stooped to look at them. One photo showed Zack, one arm wrapped around an amazingly attractive silver-haired Marie in her later years. There were several old photos of a young Zack and Marie with preteen children, in a formal pose. Another photo showed middle-aged Zack and Marie, with a show horse, receiving a huge trophy. There were Graduation pictures of children that looked very old. Some family group shots appeared to be more recent. Candid group shots taken on the farm showed children of different ages, probably grandchildren. Separate portraits of two young men in military uniforms were set apart from the rest. Jonathan searched for a photo of Betsy Baron but if it was there, he did not recognize her.

"Lots of grandchildren," Jonathan shouted down the stairs to Zack.

"Eleven," was the quick reply, "and great-grandchildren too, sixteen of them!"

Zack got up from his chair and turned on more lamps in the library. He went into adjacent rooms and soon the entire first floor glowed with an amber hue.

Grinning, Jonathan moved down the shadowy hall. Will I ever have great-grandchildren? Jonathan thought—fat chance—got to get a wife first.

A night light illuminated the attractive bathroom enough. New, unwrapped men's toiletries lay expectantly by the sink. Jonathan found himself feeling peeved again.

Jonathan dried his hands while peering out the small window. Light from downstairs reflected on the densely falling snow. Trees, a few feet from the house appeared as shadows. He uttered aloud, "Now I'll have to drive through this stuff all the way back to the city. Better finish up and hit the road."

As Jonathan opened the bathroom door, he could hear the burning wood faintly crackling and sputtering in the downstairs fireplace. A stirring nearer him in the hall startled Jonathan. He stuck his head out of the door, looking in both directions. There was no one. The air was still with the faint aroma of the fire, pipe smoke, and that fragrance. He stepped into the hall. A definite movement behind him caused Jonathan to spin around, "Zack, is that you?"

The dark hall was empty. Jonathan reeled nervously.

"You're losing it kid," he said to himself, "have to go easy on the java."

His heart was pounding as he quickly skidded down the stairs. At the bottom, he gathered composure and entered the library.

Zack was staring into the fire as Jonathan settled back down in the deep, cozy chair.

"Snowing harder," Jonathan said.

"Well over a foot already, better put your car in the garage," Zack said still staring at the fire. "With Claire away, her garage bay is empty."

"Zack, I really have to go home."

"Jonathan, you should move your car, the plow will be coming soon."

"Plow, great, I'll…"

"Hold your horses, I think you'll see there is no way you will drive in this storm tonight. You can pull your car into Claire's garage bay."

In the mudroom, Zack offered Jonathan a heavy work jacket, a hat, gloves, and a pair of old, buckle overshoes. Jonathan examined each article of clothing, bundled up, and to his surprise, everything fit.

Zack suggested that Jonathan sweep the car of snow then clear the snow from the front of the tires, and proceed in a low gear, slowly to the garage. He handed Jonathan a snow shovel and a broom, and went to open the garage door.

Jonathan trudged to his car through deep snow. Zack was right, he would not leave Redemption Ridge Farm tonight. In fact, he became concerned about moving his car at all. He shoveled a path ahead of all four tires, and swept the car. When he opened the door, it held the odor of fresh coffee. Brown ice reflected the interior light from the passenger side carpet. "Crap," he said aloud. He started the engine and slowly crept to the open garage door where Zack waited.

The four bay interior was modern, well lighted and heated. An ancient Chevrolet pickup truck in the far bay looked like it was in running condition. Next to it, a restored candy-apple-red, '39 Ford, gleamed under the bright fluorescents. A late model jeep occupied the adjacent bay.

Zack saw Jonathan's interest in the old car and truck. "Toys," he said. "The farm vehicles are in another garage. When all the kids come, they enjoy taking the Ford and Chevy into town. I still drive, the jeep is mine, but I don't use it much. Betsy uses it to shop. Claire drives a British living room."

With the exterior door closed behind them, both Zack and Jonathan examined the automobile's coffee-puddle on the carpet.

"That was what happened when Percy attacked me on the lane," Jonathan said ruefully.

Zack chuckled. "There is carpet shampoo and everything you need in the cabinets over there. You'll find a wet-vac as well. I'll see you in the house," he said, leaving Jonathan to the task.

Coffee puddle removed and carpet freshly cleaned, Jonathan left the car windows open to dry the carpet in the warmth of the garage and returned to the mudroom. He hung the loaned work jacket near Zack's and removed the overshoes.

Zack met him there.

"Ben will do his best to keep up with the storm. He will plow the lane and driveway every few hours, so you may hear him in the night. Tim is with him. I called and asked him to keep a path cleared to the barn. They'll have to come by several times before the snow stops."

"He clears the lane too, you said; maybe I can leave tonight," Jonathan suggested.

"Afraid not, radio is reporting the highways are too dangerous for travel. They are telling everyone to stay indoors so the crews can do their job."

"Maybe it will lighten up by morning," Jonathan said.

Zack ignored his inference. "Those fancy jeans of yours are wet; let me show you to the guest room. While you were cleaning the car, I pulled out some of my grandson Jack's farm clothes that he keeps here. They're clean and about your size."

No less resigned to the idea of leaving, Jonathan tagged along with Zack obediently. Annoyed or not, this man paid for Jonathan's education and he owed him for that, and probably a lot more.

The guest room was more like a hotel suite, with a king-sized bed, nightstands, desk, TV, and a comfortable reading chair. Jonathan was stunned. A pile of neatly folded clothing lay on the bed. Jonathan found pressed faded jeans, a chambray shirt, sweater, unopened packages of BVDs, and a new pair of heavy socks. On the floor, there was a box of assorted footwear and Jonathan found a pair of worn moccasins that fit.

"The bathroom in the hall is yours during your stay, no en suites in the old part of the house. This is the original master bedroom; bathrooms were added after the house was built. They are on the side toward the septic tank.

"If you need anything, chances are we have got it. A lot of family visit and clients stay while their mares are being covered. They are all used to luxury but usually forget to bring something so we keep a supply of the necessities as well as the niceties," Zack said.

Zack left Jonathan and went downstairs.

Alone in the bedroom, Jonathan surveyed his surroundings. His knees weakened, he felt nauseated and the room spun. He flopped onto the bed. Darkness descended, he imagined hearing loud cracking sounds and seeing flashes of light. Laying flat on his back, he felt the same pressure on his chest and saw the shadow image of someone standing over him.

Jonathan struggled to his feet. Guided by the night light, he staggered to the bathroom, ran cold water, and splashed his face. He leaned on the sink and stared at his dark reflection in the mirror. Before arriving at this strange place, Jonathan never knew the feeling of being out of his body, of watching everything that was happening, but being unconnected. Now the feeling was too familiar.

Jonathan dressed in the clothes Zack provided and carried his own clothes downstairs. With Zack's direction, he found the impressive laundry and dumped his designer jeans, button down Oxford, socks and unmentionables in for a swim.

Zack was back in the library; book in hand, in his fireside chair. Jonathan was happy that his host chose to maintain the fire, in this room. He had become very fond of the library's coziness. As Jonathan entered, Zack looked up.

"Is there someone else in the house?"

"No," Zack answered, a puzzled look on his face, "why do you ask?"

"I was certain that I heard someone when I was upstairs earlier; it sounded like they passed in the hall outside the bathroom."

"No. It's just the two of us."

Jonathan dropped heavily into the chair he now considered his. He looked with admiration at the old man sitting across from him, nearly a century on the planet and no signs of mental deterioration. He was physically fit and obviously happy in his own skin.

"Do you want to take a break and read for a while, or should we continue with the interview," Jonathan asked.

"We can continue."

With the tiny tape machine quietly running, Jonathan asks Zack to tell him a little about how he and Marie spent their leisure time over the years.

Zack explains that the horses started as a hobby that grew into an enjoyable business.

"Marie wanted to start a breeding program. Once all the kids were in college, we enjoyed the freedom to travel. We visited horse shows and stables around the United States, Canada, and Europe to find the perfect match of physical perfection and temperament of each horse. Marie developed a respected professional reputation for herself, the farm, and our program."

"Do all the horses in the old barn belong to you?" Jonathan asked.

Percy, the Percheron stallion belongs to us. The rest are clients' mares. They are all pregnant. After conception, some clients leave their pregnant mares with us through foaling. At the height of breeding season, the stallion is housed in a separate stable.

"What about the pregnant mares here now," Jonathan asked, "how long before they deliver?"

"Soon, the gestation period for a horse is eleven months. All competing horses are considered to have January birthdays. They are categorized by age and gender. A horse actually born in January bred for racing or showing will have an advantage over a less mature competitor born later in the year.

"We try to plan the birth date for a January or February foal. Clients' mares board here before breeding so we can watch their cycles. Later in the pregnancy, many are returned to our care when they are close to delivery."

Changing the subject using an interviewer style, in a manner he hoped would get Zack off guard Jonathan asked, "What do you attribute your long life to Zack?"

Zack answered without hesitation; "That's a question without an answer. Just more to do here I guess."

Jonathan expected Zack to give a candid claim of clean living or plenty of fiber in the diet, something fun that Jonathan could quote in the article. This was too spiritual, too philosophical, and too esoteric. Not knowing exactly how to respond, Jonathan stalled by turning over the tape in his machine.

Zack eased himself up from his chair. He walked slowly across the room as though he was going after something. Halfway across the floor the telephone rang on the table in front of him. He answered and listened quietly for a moment.

"Yes, I'm fine. I don't need anything. He is here now, yes, the writer fellow. He can help me in the barn later. No, I will not shovel … Ben and Tim are plowing through the night. We'll be fine. Okay honey. Love you too! … Yes, your sister and her friend are staying in the city at the apartment. They will meet Becky. Claire will bring her back here. You'll call Claire. Okay, when you speak to her, please tell her to stay there until the roads are safe to travel. Yes, we will trim the tree together when the whole family is here, yes, Christmas Eve. Okay, we'll talk tomorrow. Have a good night.

"That was my other daughter, Becky's mom," Zack offered as he returned to his chair. "Those girls hover around me like hens. Good girls, I'm blessed."

"Predictable too," Jonathan observed, referring to Zack's anticipation of the call. "I mean, you knew the phone was going to ring. She must call at the same time every day, huh?"

Zack looked toward the telephone, then mused, "She usually calls me in the evening, right after dinner, just called earlier today because of the storm."

Zack turned on the Albany radio station so Jonathan could hear the New York State weather forecast. The newscaster was finishing the world news. He referenced Lech Wałesa's upcoming installation as the first Polish President elected by the people. The newscaster said that the next day, Saturday, December 22, 1990, would be a pivotal date in Polish history.

The reporter gave storm related closings and cancellations. He then reminded listeners that only three shopping days remained until Christmas. There was an awkward segue when the news anchor asked the weather reporter how the snowstorm might affect late Christmas shoppers.

The weather report was dismal. State Police from New York and Massachusetts were calling in reports to the station of cars and trucks stranded in snowdrifts on highways and secondary roads. Authorities asked the station's listeners to stay off the roads. There would be several more inches of snow accumulation before the big storm ended.

Jonathan's mind was churning. So many strange things were happening. Claire left yesterday to avoid the snowstorm. Zack knew that the storm would be heavy. Why hadn't he called off the appointment and saved Jonathan the trip? It appeared that Zack actually anticipated that Jonathan would be stranded. Zack knew he would not be able to leave until the roads were cleared and even planned on his assistance with the horses. Then there was the clothing and toiletries, Jonathan felt confused and annoyed again, but he was also intrigued. Something about this house made him feel almost at home. In some ways, he didn't want to leave.

Jonathan asked for more details about Zack's early life with Marie. Zack's bright eyes squinted and his face wrinkled with delight.

"Marie was quiet, sweet, and focused. We were just about as different as any two people could be. Marie told me years later what her first impression of me was and it was not flattering. You know, things were different in those days," Zack said with scholarly authority. "Ladies were ladies, and gentlemen were gentlemen. Well, we tried to act like gentlemen. It is true that the war caused some folks to live everyday as if it was their last. Neither Marie nor I thought that way.

"When Marie and I found each other again in France years later, it was still awkward. Speaking French, I asked her if we could have a drink together. That seemed like a smooth thing to say at the time. Marie smiled a warm thank you and said, 'perhaps another time, I must return to my job,' then she turned and walked away without as much as a peek back at me. Can you believe it? We hadn't seen each other in nearly two years, there was definitely a mutual attraction and she got up and walked away.

"Come to think of it now, it might have been that cheap perfume stench I was carrying around when I came out of the fragrance factory alley—I never asked her. Anyway, I was stunned. At the same time, my heart was fuller than ever before and I kept repeating to myself, 'Zacharie Todd, you will marry this wonderful woman some day.' I watched as she entered a nearby shop. The next day I visited the shop and asked her to have lunch with me, she accepted.

"We spent every available minute together. We walked hand-in-hand all over the little town. We found quiet corners in dark cafes and talked about every subject you could imagine. Whenever we were apart, Marie's sweet face was always in my mind. I found myself anxiously waiting for the moment that I would see her again. There were so many difficulties to overcome between Marie and me before we married, and after.

"I found out later that at that time she was preparing to have her heart broken. She feared that we could never be together. We were from very different worlds. She knew that a mixed race relationship would be difficult in the United States. Yvette told me that Marie's family would never allow her to become involved with me or leave France. They planned her life and probably even picked her husband.

"I spent weeks in France to be near her and kept asking Marie to marry me. She finally agreed and we went to her parents for their blessing. It was a very bad scene. We left dejected and I feared that Marie would not go through with our marriage.

"I brought Marie to the winery to meet my friends and partners, Sam and Jean-Paul. Meeting Sam, knowing of our deep friendship, Marie realized that race would never be a concern between us."

Chapter Sixteen

Horse History

Jonathan took a sneak peek at his watch, then at the snow blowing beyond the library window. "How did you and Marie get into farming and horses?"

Zack brightened. "It was Marie's idea. She loved horses as much as I did. On one of our business trips to Europe after World War II, I looked up an expatriate pal of mine. He was with a breeding stable, bred Egyptian and Crabbet Arabian horses. They were magnificent, sturdy, and proud.

"Marie fell in love with a beautiful Crabbet filly that was for sale, we bought her, shipped her home and registered her, *Marie's Pride and Joy*. Marie boarded her with a training stable, and prepared *Pride* to show. The young horse did very well in the show ring so Marie decided to breed her. As a mare, she threw beautiful foals. We kept one colt, registered him as *M.T.'s Hermes*, after the mythical Greek god of speed and began showing him. We began visiting the horse shows with our trainer and we became hooked.

"During the war I worked with draught war horses. I fell in love with the Percheron breed. We were already into the Arabians and loved to show the horses. On one of my trips to France, I bought a young black Percheron mare. She had already been bred, and I had a chance to see the stallion. After we got her home, she threw a beautiful black filly. Percy is one of the original mare's progeny. The horse hobby was growing into a side business. That was when we decided to purchase a farm for a place to keep and train our horses.

"Marie wanted a place where she and our family would be accepted. Some Berkshire towns, in Western Massachusetts, had a reputation for racial tolerance, so we started looking for a small farm. We found this place."

"When I arrived I saw newer buildings around the property. Are they all stables?" Jonathan asked.

"This was a dairy farm with several barns and outbuildings when we bought it. It took a lot of fixing up to make it work for horses, especially accommodating the big Percherons. Some buildings needed replacement. The largest building on the property is the arena. We needed that when we employed full-time trainers. It is now used to lunge horses for exercise.

"Percherons require much larger stalls, higher overhead clearance, and much wider stalls for foaling mares. Years ago, we outfitted the original barn, where we met, for mares near delivery or horses requiring monitoring. It was easy to raise the hayloft floor to extend stall height. We took out part of one wall and added the office. It doesn't have some of the amenities of the newer stables, but it is closest to the house and the stall sizes work for both breeds and Percy.

"When we bred, trained, and showed Arabians, one of the stable buildings was exclusively for them. There was a separate one for Percherons mares with foals and geldings. There is a stallion stable and another for Arabian mares and geldings. Other buildings are for equipment and storage"

"Where are the Arabians now?"

"We haven't had an Arabian horse on the property since before Marie died. Through the 1980s, the Federal Equine Investment Tax Credit Program was very encouraging to horse owners and breeders, many fine stallions were in syndication and selling in the hundreds of thousands of dollars. We were getting older, Marie's health was failing and it was a good time to cash out of the Arabians. Marie knew the folks in the Arabian circuit and found each horse a good home."

Jonathan wanted more information about the farm so he asked, "How long has this been your home?"

"Marie and I moved here permanently in 1936. We purchased this place in 1935 with the intention of using it weekends. However, we fell in love with the farm life and moved here sooner than planned. When we bought it the main house, where we are now, and the rooms over us were the only substantial part of the original structure. It is the original house built by Emmett Morgan. The rest was 'Jerry-built,' add-ons over the decades. The attached bathrooms were crude so we installed modern plumbing in the late 1930s. We dug a large hole in the yard and used the inverted shell of an old Ford as the septic tank. It did the job for many years—now we have a conventional system, not much chance that a sewer will ever reach us here. Fixing up the place was fun. We purchased a large old house in town and tore it down for vintage materials to use here in the reconstruction.

"This was a great, healthy environment for our kids to grow up in. I enjoyed puttering around. A couple of years after World War II, shipping got back to normal, and I didn't have to be as close to the port. I kept a modest office in the city and employed good people. They serviced the US distribution interests. Most of my activities and Marie's focused on our relationship with foreign suppliers.

"It's a different world now; my grandsons run the European import business from fancy offices in midtown Manhattan. Over the years, we have sold off all our other corporate interests.

"I expect that we will keep the Percheron breeding program here as long as Percy is in favor and I am alive. I still enjoy going to the shows and keeping in touch with all the good folks we have met through the horses. After I'm gone, I have no idea what will happen to the farm. Claire says she will stay here as long as she can. She thinks that enough of the grandchildren love this place, and one of them will bring their family here to live. That would be wonderful."

Zack sprinkled in a generous supply of humorous anecdotes with each subject addressed. He talked lovingly about his marriage to Marie and about the birth of each of his children. Zack and his soul mate and life partner made many business trips to Europe and sailed together around the world. It became clear to Jonathan that his story about Zacharie Todd was indeed going to be an interesting one to tell. It would be about Marie as well, and the deep love she and Zack shared. It would also be about the important part her perspective, dedication, and support played in the success of their business ventures, their marriage, and their life. He gave insight into the different businesses he launched or invested in during his lifetime, many were related to the show horse industry.

"From the start of our married life we were a mighty team; so brave together." A broad grin stretched across his face. "Except, the day we signed and closed on this farm. Boy, were we both frightened. We stood on the front steps and looked around. Our daughter Claire said something about how big it was. When I told her it was sixty-three acres, the shock of the realization registered on every young face as well as ours. Marie and I looked at one another and laughed to cover up our uncertainty. It all worked out. Buying this place was a leap of faith that proved to be one of the best decisions of our life."

Zack was obviously reliving that moment in memory, when the young family shared their excited uncertainty on the 130-year-old stone steps. This gave Jonathan the opportunity he needed to ask more probing questions about the farm itself.

"Do you know any of the farm's history? I saw the circa 1805 plaque by the front door."

Zack knew plenty about the old farm and delighted in telling its story.

"Indeed I do. I have dug up everything I can about this place. There are plenty of stories around town to keep up interest.

Some people think the farm, and the whole of Redemption Ridge is haunted. Even today, there are reports of ghostly apparitions appearing at the base of the ridge, and sometimes around the farm."

"Haunted?" Jonathan challenged, trying to demonstrate skepticism while inwardly shuddering. The idea of spirits floating around was becoming very disturbing.

"Redemption Ridge has been the site of accidental deaths, murders, and suicides going back to the late 1700s. The original road crossed the ridge at the edges of the cliff. It was the old Indian path. Unfortunate folks crashed to their death due to weather conditions, spooked horses, blinded by the sun, or carelessly getting too close to the edge. There are the stories of star-crossed lovers leaping together off the peak. Sometimes, only one member of the jumping lovers was killed in the fall. Survivors recovered to jump again to join their lost love, seeking redemption. That is how the ridge got its name. I'm not aware of any suicides in recent years."

"The woman at the restaurant in town told me there was a murder here at the farm. Do you know anything about that?"

"Oh that was big news at the time; I read all the reports in old newspaper clippings at the town library. It happened when the second owners of the farm lived here, back in the 1850s. The newspaper editor took a special interest. He wrote the story with relish, dug into the lives of the owners before they moved here.

"A man by the name of Oakwood Wakefield was a tough, successful Albany businessman. He met a beautiful young socialite by the name of Rebecca Palmer-Wince. She bedazzled Oakwood. They were a handsome couple and stood out in Albany society. The two had a whirlwind romance and married."

Obviously, Zack enjoyed telling the story. He memorized all the names.

"Rebecca continued to be flirtatious after the marriage. Oakwood became jealous and possessive. One day he packed up Rebecca, brought her to Massachusetts and announced that this farm was her new home.

"According to reports, Oakwood tried to make Rebecca happy on the farm. He lavished her with expensive gifts, a personal maid, even a grounds keeper to maintain her flower gardens. Still, he kept Rebecca his unhappy prisoner.

"Rebecca hated the seclusion and Oakwood made it worse by forbidding her involvement in community activities. Joining him on his business trips ceased, and he only allowed Rebecca to attend church services when he was home to accompany her.

"Oakwood made periodic business trips that took him away for several days at a time, leaving Rebecca at the farm. Her only company at the house was the aging maid that Oakwood hired for her. The grounds keeper, a young man by the name of Joseph caught Rebecca's attention. In time, Rebecca and Joseph fell in love.

"Oakwood became suspicious and one day he lied about a trip, left in the morning, but returned home that night. The lovers were in his bed together when he found them. In a violent rage, he shot them both on the spot.

"The maid slept in a back room off the woodshed. In the morning, she found Oakwood dead, in front of the kitchen fireplace. He had turned the gun on himself while the lover's bodies lay cold and stiff in his bed.

"Shortly after the shooting, the children of the town started chanting.

Rebecca and Joseph were never wed,
But, they slept together in Oakwood's bed.
Oakwood came home and found them there.
Without a word, he shot them dead.
Then went to the kitchen and sat in a chair
He shot himself in deep despair.

"You might still hear this ditty repeated around town today." Zack continued. "What is it that brings people to minimize, or find humor in violent death?"

Jonathan commented, "Some psychologists maintain that humor can make a bad situation better, that it is healthy. Like the attraction to view a terrible accident, our psyche balancing out opposite traits. Kids are brought up with violent nursery rhymes. When I was young, my uncle enjoyed frightening me by reciting.

Lizzie Borden took an ax
And gave her father forty whacks.
When she saw what she had done
She gave her mother forty-one.

Zack raised one eyebrow. "I suppose there might be something to that. The Lizzie Borden murders are true Massachusetts folklore. They occurred in Fall River, in 1892—Lizzie became a celebrity."

While Zack told of Redemption Ridge's grim history, despite the whimsical ditty, Jonathan's stomach turned and he found himself catching his breath. This information was far afield of the reason for his visit, but he found it strangely riveting.

Chapter Seventeen

The Cocktail Hour

Both men sat without speaking in front of the crackling fire. Zack puffed on his pipe.

Jonathan knew Zack was thinking about Marie, the woman he loved so deeply, now separated from him by death. Jonathan was thinking about Oakwood, Rebecca and Joseph. His vision of a bloody body beside him and a dark shadow over him returned. Quietly Jonathan stood, left the library and went upstairs.

At the top of the stairs, the dim light on the credenza cast shadows across the family photos. Jonathan entered the bathroom and looked out of the window at the blowing snow. A post lamp below wore a high white cap. As Jonathan watched, it broke apart swirling in the howling wind, and disappeared.

He left the bathroom door open. Jonathan relieved himself noisily.

"What is that sweet fragrance?" Jonathan questioned aloud to Zack whose shadow was moving in the hall outside the door.

No answer.

"Hey Zack, what's that fragrance? It's kind of pretty. Zack?"

No response.

As the toilet flushed, Jonathan peered into the empty hall.

In the guest room, Jonathan sat on the bed and tried to sort the extraordinary experiences of the past several hours. Was he beginning to believe in ghosts? Was he losing his mind? Was someone playing tricks on him? He was confused. He wanted to believe that there was a rational explanation for his visions and emotional upset. He remembered reading that certain stimulus can cause hallucinations in a healthy mind. Jonathan did not want to believe Zack or anyone was intentionally hazing him, but there were indications of the possibility.

Jonathan convinced himself that despite the strangeness of the situation, the purpose and value of this meeting outweighed his concerns.

The cellular telephone Jonathan carried in his briefcase was shaped like a brick and almost as heavy. He studied the clumsy instrument for a moment, thinking, what could they have put in this thing that weighs so much?

A few years before, a cousin of Jonathan's, a physicist working in computer development, told him that one day he would carry his telephone, computer, and television in a small package the size of a cigarette pack. Jonathan looked forward to that day, when his personal phone would be small enough to carry in his pocket, or maybe on his wrist, like Dick Tracy.

The thought of the cartoon detective brought a grin to Jonathan's face. "Dick Tracy, I could use your help right now." Jonathan said aloud.

Jonathan powered up the telephone, pleased to see that he had a signal. He dialed his friend's apartment in New York.

"Hey Sue, it's Jonathan."

"Jonathan, are you home? Isn't this storm ghastly? Is everything alright?"

"That's why I called. I'm stuck in the Berkshires and don't think that I'll be back in the city in time for your dinner party."

"Oh, we already canceled. I left a message on your home phone line. The city is at a dead stop. We have rescheduled for

Christmas Eve, you can make it Christmas Eve, can't you?"

"I don't think that will be a problem. Sue?"

"Yes."

"Will your friend from the office and her daughter still be joining us?"

"Yes, they haven't any other plans and they are thrilled to be partying on Christmas Eve."

"This may sound strange, but do you know what hair color your friend's daughter has?"

"Yes, Jonathan, that is a strange question, and no, I don't know the color of her hair—why?"

"Do you think she is a blonde?"

"Men," Sue said mockingly, "I don't know, Jonathan. I have only met her mother. Why would you ask such a silly question?"

"It isn't what you think. I'll explain when I see you."

Paper rustled on Sue's end of the line. "Wait, I just found my note here. I have the daughter's name." Sue spelled it for Jonathan, "It's A-S-H-I-A, Ashia! By the sound of her name, my guess is she is not a light-haired person. I know Mrs. Scott is very Anglo, but as I recall she told me her husband's mother was from the Middle East.

"What's this about Jonathan, are you going to get picky on me. I am trying to find a nice woman for you but I am not going to get pedigrees."

Jonathan laughed. "Sue, I can hardly wait until I tell you about this trip, and no, I am not getting picky. Got to go. I'll call you when I'm back in town."

Zack was gone when Jonathan returned to the library. He heard noises in the kitchen, something smelled delicious and Jonathan followed his nose.

"What's cooking?" Jonathan asked, his stomach beginning to grumble.

"Right now it's sliced baguettes toasting in the oven. I made a Bruschetta topping yesterday and let it blend in the icebox overnight," Zack said. "We have time for cocktails before we do the chores."

Jonathan found the dated term, "ice box," humorous. He found the phrase, "do the chores," daunting. When he sniffed the mixture that Zack spooned into two large ramekins, he forgot everything else.

"Tomatoes, onions, garlic, and something else...?"

Zack looked straight into Jonathan's eyes and stated authoritatively, "Finely chopped tomatoes, onions, and garlic if you please! And, finely chopped black and green olives with a touch of extra virgin olive oil, a dash of grated Parmesan cheese. The mixture should have the consistency of fine caviar. It is the only way to be sure all the ingredients are blended into every bite. It might not be considered the traditional recipe, but wait until you taste it."

A kitchen-convenient temperature control wine cellar with a glass door sat under one of the counters. With the practiced ease of decades of experience, Zack selected a dark bottle, removed the cork, and placed it on the counter. He took crystal goblets from a suspension rack and put them next to the bottle.

"Have you done much wine tasting, Jonathan?"

"Only faking it to impress a date."

"Well, let's taste this together."

Zack poured two glasses half-full of the crimson beverage. He took a pad of white paper from a drawer and handed it to Jonathan.

"Hold your glass in front of the paper. What color is the wine?"

"Red." Jonathan remarked immediately.

"Look again. Is it maroon, purple, ruby, garnet, red, brick, or brownish?

"I'm not that familiar with the differences of the color red. It isn't purple and it isn't brown."

"Lesson one. The color tells the age of the wine. An older red wine will often have more orange tinges on the edges than younger red wines. Older white wines are darker, than younger white wines when comparing the same variety at different ages."

"I don't think that I have ever seen a brown wine, so I take it that brown isn't good."

"What else do you see? Is it opaque, translucent, watery, or dark?"

"Translucent I think, and it is clear."

"Okay, so it isn't cloudy. Is it dull or brilliant?"

"Brilliant."

"Good. Tilt your glass and give it a little swirl—is there sediment, bits of cork, or anything floating?"

"Looks good to me."

"Now to really impress your date, swirl your glass and count to ten to yourself. This vaporizes the wine's alcohol and releases more aromas."

Jonathan was enjoying the lesson and followed directions to the letter, bobbing his head up and down with each count to ten.

Zack stifled a laugh, "Avoid the head bobbing if you really want to impress the date, Jonathan. Now, take a quick whiff to gain a first impression."

Jonathan dutifully whiffed.

"Stick your nose into the glass and inhale through your nose. A wine's aroma is an excellent indicator of quality and characteristics. Swirl the wine and let the aromas mix and sniff it again. Does it smell like oak, berry, flowers, vanilla, or citrus?"

"When do I get to drink it?"

"You can only perceive four tastes—sweet, sour, bitter, and salt. The average person can smell some two thousand different scents, and wine has over a couple of hundred. Smell the wine three times. The third smell usually gives you more information than the first. The *nose* is a word wine tasters use to describe the bouquet and aroma. Pinpointing the *nose* helps you identify certain characteristics.

"The best way to learn your own preferences of wine is to memorize the smell of the individual grape varieties. For white, just try to memorize the three major grape varieties: Chardonnay, Sauvignon Blanc, and Riesling. Keep smelling them and smelling them until you can identify the differences, one from the other. For the reds, it is a bit more difficult, but you can still take three major grape varieties: Pinot Noir, Merlot, and Cabernet

Sauvignon. Try to memorize those smells."

"Are there negative smells?"

"You'll recognize vinegar, sulphur, and cork. Cork is like a musty cellar. Wine will absorb the smell of a bad cork."

"Sulphur, how would that happen?"

"Sulphur dioxide kills bacteria in wine, prevents unwanted fermentation, and acts as a preservative. It can cause a burning or itching feeling in your nose if it's overused."

"Can I drink it now?"

Zack nodded.

"Mmmmmm, I like it, that's good."

"That is the most important point. Enjoy wine."

"Do you do this every time you open a bottle of wine?"

"Not really. When I open a bottle for myself, I just sniff and pour. If I don't like the smell or color I toss it out and open another."

Jonathan tucked the wine bottle under his arm and carried the glasses to the table. Zack removed the toast from the oven. He topped a crusty medallion with the mixture and handed it to Jonathan.

With eyes closed, Jonathan savored the new treat and hummed, "The taste is unbelievable."

They used long-handled spoons to pile the aromatic mixture on the toasted bread.

"A few days here and I won't fit into my clothes."

"A few days here, my boy, and we work off any excess pounds. Today was easy. Wait until morning. It's only you and me to muck the stalls. Percy eats enough for four and he is a fine-tuned manure machine."

Jonathan rolled his eyes to the heavens, assembled another Bruschetta, and followed it with a taste of the robust red wine.

"So, you have become a wine connoisseur as well as an importer?"

"I'm hardly a wine aficionado. As far as taste buds are concerned, I like my pipe and this heavy garlic-flavored creation we are munching. It's difficult to imagine how discriminating a smoker or garlic eater can be about their wine."

After cocktails, Zack served lemon orzo with chicken cutlet sautéed with fresh mushrooms in a white wine and capers sauce. During dinner, the two men chatted about life in New York City.

"I understand the Central Park Conservancy restored the old Carousel this year," Zack said. "Have you seen it?"

"Yes, they did a great job and the area around the Carousel has been improved. Why is that important to you?"

"Memories," Zack responded.

"Marie, the kids, and I spent a lot of time there as a young family. A mule under the platform drove the original Carousel then. It upset Marie; she thought that it was cruel treatment of the animal. That was my Marie. Whenever we went into the city, Marie would act as our activities director. The trip to the city would include something for the kids, like the Carousel, but it would also include a theater matinee and either a ballet, opera, or symphony in the evening."

"Marie sounds like she was an extraordinary woman," Jonathan remarked.

"That she was. She was interested in everybody she met and many she never met. Marie was accepting, open-minded, and gave everyone the benefit of the doubt."

"You have sophisticated taste. Living here, so far removed from the cultural activities of the metropolis, I would have thought you would prefer city life." Jonathan said.

"We have kept an apartment in Manhattan for business and pleasure through the years, and if we crave an international flavor, it is an easy drive to Montreal. Since living here, we have never been far from entertainment. Albany, Springfield, and Pittsfield are near enough. When we moved here, in the 30s, the big name entertainers came to us, vaudeville was big at the Court Square Theater in Springfield. We saw Abbot and Costello, Amos and Andy, Bob Hope—major entertainment in Albany. There was dancing to the big bands, and floorshows at nightclubs. In summer, there are professional performances at Tanglewood and Jacob's Pillow. The Eastern States Exposition grounds are nearby and there are several horse shows there as well as the annual fair.

When my boys were growing up, we had minor league baseball. After the Massachusetts Turnpike opened, we could be in Boston in a couple of hours. You may have already guessed from my favorite hat that I am a Red Sox fan. Our life here has been very good."

Curious about the eerier image of the farm, Jonathan said, "The restaurant waitress in town told me there is a man's face on the vertical surface of the Redemption Ridge. I tried to see it when we were coming back to the house, but the snow was too dense."

"Oh yes, at certain times shadows make it very obvious. That adds to the supernatural speculation around here."

"You mentioned that this house is considered haunted. Do you think the farm is haunted?"

"This is very far afield from a business interview. I'm not sure how you will present any answer that I give you when you write your piece."

"Zack, I'm just curious. This is for me, strictly off the record."

"To be honest, Jonathan, accepting the existence of ghosts is difficult for me."

"You make it sound like you might be open to the possibility. Did Marie believe in ghosts?"

"Let's say that Marie and I never accepted the idea of spirits coming back to haunt, or cause problems for the living. Marie and I shared the belief we humans have a soul and that soul will exist after the body dies. It's hard for me to grasp the possibility of spirit entities moving things around, clanking chains, or dragging humans into an underworld. What I can relate to is communication at some level between a soul in a human experience and another on the other side, a kind of ESP if you want to call it that. That is what I feel happens when a psychic accurately delivers information and predictions. Marie was very intuitive. She amazed me with some of the predictions she made over the years. I have to acknowledge there must be some connection.

"Marie taught me to be open to all possibilities. An afterlife is one of them. As to haunting, the stories about Resurrection Ridge all seem to focus on a force that turns a negative to a positive. That's where the redemption reference comes in.

"Marie was on a constant spiritual journey. She remained an active church-attending Catholic, but her beliefs extended to the metaphysical and included reincarnation. She found peace in her beliefs, never feared death, and seemed to me to have a unique knowing.

"I have seen so many changes that improved human understanding. There have been innumerable scientific discoveries and paradigm shifts during my lifetime. Metaphysical concepts, even resources that I scoffed at decades ago when Marie brought them to my attention, are now accepted as fact.

"That first book about life after death started Marie on a search. Over the years, she grew to believe that each soul grows as they journey through many incarnations. She believed some incarnations to be in human form, on this earth, and in another form elsewhere or on a different plane in between. She told me once that the majority of the world's population believes in reincarnation. I have to admit that through the years, Marie presented plausible arguments in favor of multiple lives, but I have been slow to become a true believer. I don't relate to the idea, and have never really gotten into it." Zack acted disturbed. "Sorry now, that I ever did anything that upset Marie. She was so good."

Jonathan detected tears in the old man's eyes.

Chapter Eighteen

Friday Evening in the Barn

The two men efficiently cleaned the kitchen together after dinner. The grandfather clock in the front hall chimed, it was time to feed and water the animals, and to prepare them for the night.

The swirling snow continued as Zack and Jonathan trudged heads down to the barn. Homer jogged alongside periodically demonstrating his snowflake snapping expertise.

Ben had cleared the path, driveway, and the area in front of the barn door. With both men pushing the door, it slid open easily.

If horses had hands, the two men would have received a round of applause. However, the warm greeting quickly turned to grumbled impatience until Zack measured out grain to the last member of the snorting bunch.

Both cats came to life and followed Zack's every move, repeatedly rubbing against his legs.

"What are the cats' names?"

"One is Growltiger, the other is Etcetera."

Jonathan laughed, "Broadway show cats, that's interesting, do they sing?"

"There is a bag of dry cat food and a bowl in the grain box, shake some into their bowl and they'll sing for you."

"I thought barn cats ate mice."

"Feeding them keeps them healthy, they are still great mousers, they love to hunt."

"Which one is Growltiger?"

"The male."

"Thanks, that's a big help."

The sound of their food bag opening drew the cats. They both chinned Jonathan's legs while he filled the small bowl.

"Why do they do that?" Jonathan asked about the attention his legs were getting.

"They like you and they are making you one of them."

"Great."

With Zack's direction, Jonathan began filling each horse's water bucket. The water hose was reeled into an enclosed fireproof box with a small heater coil to keep it from freezing. Water flowed from a tap that looked like a regular hose bib. Zack explained that it was a lawn hydrant designed to keep the water in the ground well below the frost line when not in use.

"Where is the cat's water bowl?" Jonathan asked.

"A small amount of water will freeze quickly. It's easy enough for them to drink from the horses' water buckets."

There was no end to what Jonathan was learning on this trip. The experience reminded Jonathan of the stable in the city and his short-term romance. He had to admit that it was really a physical thing. Priscilla looked great bouncing in the saddle in form-fitting riding clothes.

With the sound of munching and rustling in the background, Zack and Jonathan sat together on a wide bench. The horses' body heat as well as their own, generated from physical activity, made it comfortable. Zack wanted to be sure that everything was okay before they left.

Listening to the barn sounds caused Jonathan's mind to drift.

He imagined himself kneeling in a darkened stall holding down the head of an agitated mare in obvious labor. Muffled grunts came from her as she delivered a foal. Two men, their faces shadowed, were pulling the foal free. A husky woman, wrapped in heavy scarves and a cloak, held a flickering lantern high. Its orange flame reflected in the frightened eyes of the anxious horse. The shadows played on the men, the stall walls, and the straw-strewn floor.

It was so real. Jonathan could smell the straw and birth odor. He could feel his own anxiety easing, as he knew that the delivery was going to be trouble free.

"Ah, she's a fine one that filly, going to be like her mom." The woman said with an Irish lilt.

They all stood back while the mare cleaned the newborn and poked it up onto wobbly legs.

"You should all get some rest," one of the men said as he wiped his hands. "I'll stay with them till morning."

"Yes, I'll be back then," Jonathan said and opened his eyes.

"Where did you go?" Zack asked. "You were moving around and talking to yourself."

Jonathan stood and looked at the bench in an effort to change the subject, but a closer look at the patina actually captivated him. He stroked the wood, "This is very nice, and it looks old!"

Zack put a gloved hand on the bench. "When we bought the place it was in the gazebo. Marie replaced it with a glider settee. She thought the bench had spent enough time in the weather and that the protection of the barn would be a better home."

"Glider settee?"

"It's a bench that floats back and forth from a suspension, a rocker that doesn't rock."

Another chuckle from the mustachioed curmudgeon—he was having fun with Jonathan.

"So, how old do you think this bench is?" Jonathan asked.

"It was probably made the same time the gazebo was built. It is oak, the same as the gazebo. Whoever made it wanted it to last forever, probably the man who built the house."

Jonathan rubbed his hand over the worn finish and imagined smelling the fresh sawed wood. *I will sit here holding each of my children someday*, Jonathan thought.

Every time Jonathan had a flight of fantasy, he tried hard to return to the purpose of his visit.

"How about World War II? It must have affected your import business. It certainly upset shipping."

Zack was quiet a long time. When he spoke, his words were soft. "In 1939 the bottom fell out of our business, again. Europe was in turmoil, shipping by sea became nearly impossible and once the United States entered World War II all focus was on military needs.

"German submarines were torpedoing transport ships and mercilessly killing innocent civilians. The age limits for the draft in 1942 extended to forty-five. For the Brits, it extended to age sixty. I was thirty-nine, but that didn't matter, I wanted to enlist anyway.

"Some of my pals went over to the Mediterranean Theater, others the South Pacific. I served here in the States. Admittedly, I didn't mind missing the action and I was able to keep in touch with some business interests."

The old man got lost in thought.

Jonathan said, "War changes a person's perspective. It seems that your experiences, still occupy your thoughts."

"Both my sons spent time in active military service in Korea, one of them was in a prisoner-of-war camp. It took years for him to get over that experience. My grandson, Michael, came home crippled from Vietnam to the flagrant disrespect from contemporaries who enjoyed the freedom their Vietnam veteran brothers fought to protect. Young Americans, holding flowers and preaching love, hid from responsibility and broke the law. They treated every returning soldier as though they were party to the My Lai Massacre.

"There were 105 US soldiers involved at My Lai. It was horrendous and unforgivable. Worse still was that it left a terrible scar on all of our military, and gave an excuse for radical behavior by dissenters. Vietnam vets faced abuse, were called baby-killers and treated like the enemy.

"It filled me with rage to see reports of *peace-lovers* and *flower children* spitting on the caskets of dead teenagers who paid for our freedom with their lives. They were more interested in protecting a tree and went into forests to set traps that would maim or kill innocent Americans, working to support their families." Zack flushed with anger. His thoughts seemed to surge through him. Zack stood abruptly. His movement caught the attention of one of the mares. Her eyes rolled and she stretched a thick neck into the aisle. She appeared to be concerned.

Zack moved to the mare and stroked the massive head, he continued, "When my grandson Michael visits, he arrives in a special van designed for his wheelchair. You might think he would be angry. In Vietnam, he fought in a war that many Americans did not believe in. However, Michael has never complained about losing his legs, or the terrible treatment he received in the years after his return. He learned a great deal about human suffering in a Vietnamese jungle and in hospitals. He is one of the most compassionate men you will ever meet.

"Michael entered the war from college and received a direct commission. He told me about several discussions he had with career officers. They were not the trigger-happy warriors the media and motion pictures portray them to be. The officers were well schooled in strategic and operational leadership; but what impressed Michael most was their compassion and sensitivity."

Jonathan contemplated what Zack said and offered, "By the nature of military service, a military career must contribute a great deal to understanding human suffering."

Zack nodded, patted the big horse's head and spoke to her softly before he continued.

"Michael communicates with many of the men and women he served with in Vietnam and met in the veteran's hospitals. In fact, whenever he visits, he makes it a point to go to the VA Hospital here; it is nearby. As a journalist, you should see for yourself how these poor souls' lives have been ravaged. Marie and I have volunteered there since the late 30s, shortly after we moved into this house. We met World War I veterans who never saw combat. You never hear anything about them. They were victims of sabotage. Many were only seventeen years old when their lives stopped, their brains chemically altered by enemy-sympathizing doctors.

"The vast majority of Vietnam Vets that Michael knows returned to their communities as valued contributors."

Jonathan joined Zack beside the mare, her eyes closed, enjoying Zack's attention.

"May I ask you about your interracial marriage? I have no idea how a mixed race marriage was viewed decades ago. In addition, having a black business partner certainly was rare. I'm sure the three of you encountered a lot of bigotry through the years, how did you handle it?"

"When the three of us traveled together I think most people thought that Sam and Marie were the couple and we allowed them to think that if it was convenient.

"Sam, Marie, and I had some difficulties with prejudices along the way. Marie and I faced some very tough times when just the two of us traveled together. More trouble in parts of this country than when we traveled outside the States. There were many raised eyebrows when we entered a restaurant or a theater. We had no choice but to deal with it.

"It was one of the reasons Marie and I bought this farm, in this town. We faced reality. This area was known to be more racially tolerant, and the seclusion suited our style. Little by little, we became accepted socially. As the years passed, our circle of close friends expanded. Our kids never had any real problems growing up. They always had healthy complexions, but I suppose that was attributed to their life on the farm."

"Did the experience motivate you to support racial causes?"

"If you mean did we join the NAACP, in a way, we supported the cause financially. Terrible things were happening to black people. We saw prejudice first-hand and we helped a little when the NAACP started 'Crisis'—you know, the organization's magazine.

Zack gazed into space. "I haven't thought much about that for some time. Not since Marie died. That brings back memories. William DuBois, one of the founders of the NAACP was born near here in Great Barrington in the late 1800s. His family was one of only a few Negroes in that community at the time. He also worked in the mills at one time. William was a go-getter. He earned his PhD at Harvard. He might have been the first black American to earn a PhD at Harvard. DuBois became an outspoken civil rights leader of his time."

"I've read about him. Did you know him personally?"

"Sure, we met in the 20s, years after the NAACP was formed. William and I never really got to know one another. We probably would not have gotten along at all if we did. He was an intellectual; I was not. I don't think he agreed with my capitalist philosophy. He was much older than I was, and we did not see eye to eye on a lot of things.

"What DuBois was doing for Negroes was important and good, so Marie and I offered what support we could. He changed history. Personally, I admired Dr. King's approach. King seemed more like Gandi. However, he came along a lot later.

"DuBois was controversial," Zack continued, "he left the NAACP in the 30s. He was a Socialist you know. In the 50s, he was a target of McCarthyism and indicted as an agent for the Soviet Union but he was acquitted. I believe that he openly joined the Communist Party after that, sometime in the early 60s."

Jonathan wagged his pen in the air, "I remember studying the NAACP for a paper I was writing. I read about William DuBois. As I recall, he moved to Ghana and became a naturalized citizen before he died."

"Yes, now that you mention it, I think that Marie told me that, she kept in touch with him after he left this country."

"I would like to know a little about your politics. What is your political ideology—if I may ask?"

"As a war-tempered young buck married to a colored woman starting a foreign import business, you would have to say my ideology has always been very convoluted," Zack said.

"If you are as generous in your support of social causes as many people think, you must be a liberal," Jonathan commented.

"I didn't realize that many people know I exist. I try to keep a very low profile. Your conclusion smacks of bias, Jonathan, are you inferring that only liberals support social causes?"

"I meant politically. Are you a liberal?"

"You see how politics distorts fact. I know many professed political liberals who are far from being generous when it comes to sharing their personal wealth. Moreover, I know many political conservatives who are quiet, generous, philanthropists.

"Politically, I am a fiscal conservative. In my experience, everything goes better when the government stays out of the way. Politicians push entitlement programs that buy them votes and the programs breed dependency. That does not mean that I am insensitive or lack compassion. I believe that the strong should take care of the weak, the young, the elderly, and the ill, but handouts do not build self-reliance, or self-respect."

"Do you think that all politicians pander for votes?"

"Seeking political office, gaining it, and staying there is expensive. A true accounting would probably show up on the GDP. It's a wonder that any politician has time to address important issues given the obligations they truck with them. The required payback is astronomical. Politicians cannot afford to bite the hand that feeds them, and when possible they try to turn it around so it is their hand doing the feeding. It is part of the game."

"How do you feel about our current president? Do you like him?"

"I don't know him well enough to have a personal opinion. If I did, liking him should not enter into my feelings about what he brings to the job of leading the country. My position on his value to the country will be stated in the voting booth if there is a reelection bid."

"Back to the speculation of your generosity, you don't deny that you are a philanthropist, do you?"

"Marie was the ultimate humanitarian. She pointed out to me that philanthropy means the love of humanity," Zack stared at

Jonathan. "I told her that if that is the meaning of philanthropy, we should all be philanthropists. When we had enough extra capital to share, we did. However, I did not want to do anything that drew attention to our family or me. Marie explained that she could keep our identities unknown. She was totally in charge of that. After she died, our attorneys started working with my granddaughter Becky. Becky was Marie's protégé, her choice to take over that responsibility."

"You don't appear to be shy, why have you avoided the limelight all of your life?"

"To me that kind of attention demeans the purpose. Over the years I have seen power-hungry people flaunt their philanthropy publicly, while they used their influence to advance less reputable personal agendas."

"The name of the trust that paid for my scholarship, 'P.I.F.' are not your initials or Marie's. What do they stand for?"

"Pay It Forward, that's what Marie called it."

"You paid for my education without really knowing me, you contribute to worthwhile causes. Pardon my bluntness, but you must have some self-interest. What is your motivation?"

"It just seems like the right thing to do."

"That's it?"

"Jonathan, when Marie was alive she was a great teacher. She helped me understand that we each have a purpose on this earth. She helped me recognize that by allowing my conscience to be my guide I would avoid regret."

Jonathan referred to his notes. "You said you and Marie were married in a Catholic Church. You also said that Marie was a practicing Roman Catholic and that she believed in reincarnation. Did she subscribe to Irenaean theodicy? What about you, I'm curious, do you believe in reincarnation? Did you both stay in the Church through the years?"

"You make it sound like belief in reincarnation is not theological. Billions of humans on this earth believe in reincarnation. The fact that we embrace the concept of a spiritual existence after the human body dies is not unique. Belief in an experience after death is common through most religions and spiritual beliefs.

"Understanding the intellectual level of the masses in the early days of Christianity, a belief in reincarnation would have interfered with Roman Catholic Hierarchy's attempt to dominate and control the people of that time. We know that the Christian Bible makes no mention of reincarnation, and we know it has been edited and rewritten numerous times. It is possible that there was an intentional omission of reincarnation.

"Marie's personal spiritual beliefs expanded through her life. She chose to attend a Roman Catholic Church. She said that there was something mystical about being in a church full of believers praying. It made her feel closer to her personal God. My family brought me up as a Roman Catholic. I am a Christian who prefers not to participate in the Roman Catholic Celebration of the Mass and subscribes to personal beliefs over fundamentalist doctrine. In the eyes of the Church, I am a heretic. My personal God loves. I never challenged others for their beliefs or apostolate mine.

"Marie continually studied material about every religion, philosophy, and spiritual concept she could find. When she was young, she developed an interest in the writings of Immanuel Kant. As time went on her interest in metaphysical philosophy grew. She explored psychic experiences and visited the Association of Research and Enlightenment. She met Edgar Casey, corresponded with Charles and Myrtle Fillmore, Mary Baker Eddy, and a few more who shared her diverse spiritual interests.

"I have nothing against the teachings of the Church. The Church teaches that all life is sacred. I feel that way. I believe every human being has the right to life and that the taking of a life is wrong. If being a theist guides us to protect life, born or unborn, that cannot be bad. Marie and I both believed that each soul is created with a spark of the divine, denying any human being the opportunity to find their way, spiritually, just seems wrong."

With eyes glistening, Zack continued, "I fear our world is in a state of moral decay. Seeing so many die needlessly in war, then seeing so many beautiful children, grandchildren, and great grandchildren of my own come along has made me anxious for their future.

"Marie saw death in war more often and closer than I did. She carried those memories, and believing in reincarnation helped her cope. She believed that a soul reincarnates for its own growth and to assist other souls' growth, she agreed with the Church's position against abortion. She believed that every incarnating soul should have the right to a full life experience."

"What about a woman's right to her own body?"

"That is as personal as any decision gets. It is between the woman and her conscience. Far be it from me to judge. Marie didn't judge either. She certainly didn't think that court judges have the right to decide when life occurs in the womb or if a soul exists."

"So, you believe in an afterlife and a personal God?"

"When I look around I am certain that there is a greater intelligence. This universe is just too complex to be happenstance."

"But you do not belong to any church. You didn't share Marie's feelings of participation in an organized religion."

"Over the years I drifted from the Church, maybe because my head was filled with other interests—with building businesses."

"Are you saying that money became your god?"

Zack thought for a moment.

"No, it never was about the money. Oh, Marie and I enjoyed what came with it. Ours was a much better life because of our wealth, but wealth was never the goal. No, my motivation was building something that could be shared. From the beginning, seeing the products we imported arrive and go off to the marketplace was rewarding and satisfying. I thought about the Europeans, the French, and Brits who had their homes destroyed and their lives shattered by wars. I witnessed how hard they fought for their freedom. They deserved the opportunity to recover their lives. By purchasing the products they produced; wines from France, candy and cheese from Europe, fabrics from Great Britain, I was part of helping them to rebuild their lives."

Chapter Nineteen

More of Zack's Personal Philosophy

The snow continued to swirl outside, but Jonathan had forgotten about it. "Do you think the import business is good for America? Some people think that this country is importing too much, and not producing enough tangible products for export."

"You must not be one of them; I noticed the car you drove here is an import. As far as the balance of trade is concerned, I'll leave that to the economists to decide. You're a Wharton MBA, what do you think?"

"No you don't. This interview is about you!"

Zack chortled and gave Jonathan a mischievous glance, "As a business school graduate you must know that our government's initial operating revenue came from import tariffs before taxes."

"Yes, but circumstances have changed over the years. Do you think importing has gotten lopsided, what about now? Are low-priced foreign goods destroying a fair market for American manufacturers?"

His head back looking at the ceiling, Zack remained thoughtful for a few moments before speaking.

"Three years ago, in 1987, we had a global stock market crash. Recovery has been slow and now, in 1990, we are in an economic recession. Are foreign imports to blame for our America's economic woes? We have become a global marketplace. Perhaps we should address the question of why domestic and foreign markets are not purchasing American-made products. Everyone wants to find the lowest price product. The American consumer is the driving force of our US market. If we all were willing to pay for a quality product produced by an American at American wage scale, the trend would be different."

Zack continued, "Recently I read that the employee parking lots of most American factories are filled with foreign-made vehicles. The other day a union plumber came to make a repair here. He used tools made in Taiwan. He gave me a promotional ballpoint pen with his name and telephone number on it that was made in Mexico; he drove away in a Japanese truck.

"When I started importing, my company distributed products that served both the foreign and US markets. The purchase price of my foreign imports was a fraction of the cost of the final product sold here in the States.

"Many American businesses continue to grow and prosper in the distribution of foreign imports. Think about it, warehousing and sales outlets require construction, maintenance, and contribute to local employment and tax revenue. Sea and land transport is a major industry.

"In the case of alcoholic beverages, they are taxed and re-taxed from import through each sale. This year, US Custom tariff on imported brandy could go as high as 300 percent. A glass of wine in a restaurant is taxed additionally in some cities, as high as 10 percent by the local authority.

"What is fair? I've spent a lifetime trying to be fair to others and to myself. I have to do some deep soul searching to be sure that I am being honest with myself. We hear it said that fair is only fair when it is fair to all. Keeping a balance in life is very difficult to do," Zack said thoughtfully. "To keep myself in check I have a mental image of a balance scale, the scale of justice."

Zack held palms up in front of him and rocked them as an imitation of the scale seeking balance.

"Yeah, I've got the picture."

Zack went on metaphorically, "To maintain balance, the weight on each side has to be adjusted slowly and carefully. Put too heavy a weight on one side, it hits bottom. If you want to add to one side, you have to take from the other, slowly, carefully, thoughtfully. It is an interesting exercise. Adding is not difficult; deciding what has to be removed is hard."

Jonathan watched Zack, he knew a thought about Marie had entered Zack's mind; the old man's face glowed.

"Many years ago, Marie and I attended a lecture together about the 'Chaos Theory.' The speaker mentioned the often-referenced *butterfly effect*. You know, *when a butterfly flutters its wings in the Brazilian Rain Forest it affects the weather in Central Park*. That concept affected both Marie and me, the oneness of our world. We began to understand that even the smallest actions of an individual taken in the past in a remote part of the world could dramatically affect the future in a distant place. Wars are a good example of the negative. That places a heavy responsibility on each one of us."

"I believe that we are responsible to maintain balance, in our lives and in the manner that we affect our community, even the world. As I have said, sometimes that means being benevolent. Sometimes it means making tough, personal, judgmental calls," Zack said in a low whisper. He looked away.

"Can you give me an example?"

After a moment of thought, Zack said, "Mother Teresa is considered to be a great humanitarian," he gave Jonathan a penetrating look, "yet, when an ill person in her care recovers, they are returned to the streets of Calcutta to shift for themselves. Is Mother Teresa a saint for caring for the ill or a sinner for abandoning the poor, cured?"

Zack looked Jonathan in the eye and as an aside offered, "Balance, to my mind Mother Teresa is a pragmatist. Marie and I met her once and Marie supported Mother Teresa's Mission of Charity. The woman herself had quite a personal story. Marie told me Mother Teresa was only seven when her father died, probably poisoned for his political beliefs. Despite the trauma in her life that would have derailed another person, she developed a sense of service, answered the call to the Church at eighteen, received an education, and was ultimately motivated to her destiny after a visit to Darjeeling.

"I use the story to illustrate balance. Many such people have contributed in wonderful ways. Mother Teresa had given herself to the Church and needed permission from the Pope to leave her order and operate independently. You have to marvel at the fortitude of the young woman, in those years, launching such an undertaking!" Zack grinned and shook his head in a demonstration of appreciation.

"Even before addressing the practical challenges of setting up a clinic, Mother went to nursing school. She showed maturity and good judgment at a very young age, and a realistic understanding of what was necessary to prepare her for the tasks ahead."

"Have you patterned your approach to life after people you admire?"

Zack stepped back and sized up Jonathan with appreciation. "You are very good at what you do. I guess I never took a good look at myself in that way. Yes, I admire people who weigh options in favor of magnanimous benefits," Zack said, "and are willing to work to achieve their goals. I do admire people who have the courage of their convictions."

Zack relaxed his body and said, "Much of who I have become is the result of Marie's example. I so admired my Marie. She was a wonderful teacher. She was naturally intuitive, and she grasped the importance of issues quickly. I missed a formal education by leaving school in the ninth grade to go to work at the mills. Then the war came along. After the war, my energy went into my business interests."

"You are obviously well-read and have a great deal of life experience. You have lived through what may arguably be the years of greatest concentrated change in recorded history. You and Marie traveled extensively; you got to know famous people. Are there any people, places, or events that stand out in your memory?"

"Marie and I often talked about the events we witnessed together. As far as standing out, there have been so many. The memories that most quickly come to mind relate to wars. We both were sickened each time war was declared, elated when peace returned.

"Important medical breakthroughs certainly are impressive. Many horrible diseases have been cured, some eliminated. For us, the Civil Rights movement, seeing segregation ruled illegal was major.

"Man in space and on the moon is exciting. We huddled by a radio when Alan Shepard made the first suborbital space flight. The horrible Challenger Space Shuttle explosion occurred while Marie was in the hospital. It was one of the last major news events we shared together.

"When we had children, both Marie and I vowed to see to a good education for each of them. After World War II, when our youngest left home, Marie went to college. She earned her BA in History from Russell Sage.

"We would talk for hours about national and international affairs. It amazed me how history keeps repeating itself. Intelligent leaders, politicians, and business people repeating errors of the past. Why are we humans so bent on trying to make things turn out differently despite evidence to the contrary?

"I remember talking to a young man, once, about a business loan that he wanted. Young Bruce came to me because the banks wouldn't talk to him. His father died and Bruce took over the family business. He wanted me to finance an expansion. At first meeting, I was impressed. He was bright, eager, and well-educated. As we talked, he admitted he had never worked with his father in the family business. After prep school, Bruce attended college, then graduate school. During summers, he traveled. His dad fell ill and died. Without any experience or understanding, he took over the family business after receiving his MBA.

"Bruce brought me an impressive business plan for expansion. I asked if he had discussed any of his ideas with his father before the man died. He had, and told me his father told him that through the years, he tried a number of the same ideas and detailed his experiences. As a result, the father did not proceed with the business expansion.

"I asked the young man if his father didn't think the expansion would work, why did he think it would? The young man said, 'The business belongs to me, I have every right to make my own mistakes.'"

"Did you give him the loan?"

"The kid was an unharnessed, immature ego; of course I didn't give him the loan. He had years of his father's hard-earned experience to benefit from, dedicated employees to help guide him, and the company history. What I saw was a successful business, on the right track, keeping up with market growth. I told the kid to sell the business and get some good investment counseling."

"Did he take your advice and sell the business?" Jonathan asked.

"As a matter of fact everything worked out all right. The young man could not get the money for expansion so he was forced to operate the business as his father had. In time, he saw first hand, and understood what his father knew. He let the business grow naturally."

"So you don't think change is always good, and you are not above harsh criticism," Jonathan said with a wide grin.

"I believe that people learn best from personal experience, and even more from painful experience. If the kid tried what he proposed, it's likely everything his father accomplished would have been destroyed. For the sake of the employees and others who depend upon that business I hope the kid stays clear-headed. A good business with a solid foundation will grow with a growing market. The trick is to recognize opportunity and seize it, without overshooting a reachable target."

The barn noise reduced to quiet rustle and snorts. Zack said, "Let's go back to the house for a night cap." They headed for the door.

Chapter Twenty

The Chest in the Attic

Both men were exhausted and didn't speak as they each nursed a brandy in the library. When the clock in the hall struck ten, Zack stood and said, "Going to hit the hay. If you need anything, my room is at the top of the rear staircase, off the kitchen. Claire's room bisects the house and she keeps her doors locked when we have guests, but you have the run of this part of the house. I'll knock on your door in the morning, about 5:30."

He closed the vents on the fireplace screen and the remaining flame died to a glow.

Too tired to try to talk Zack into letting him sleep in the morning Jonathan nodded acceptance as each headed off to their respective rooms.

New pajamas were in their wrapping on the dresser, but Jonathan preferred sleeping in his shorts. He pulled back the covers and fell into bed.

Jonathan placed his watch on the bedside table, switched off the lamp, and settled between the crisp sheets. Soon he slipped into restless sleep.

Zack, with Homer trailing behind went to his room. He enjoyed the ritual of watching Homer circling the big padded basket in the corner of the room before plopping down. He put on pajamas, sat at the edge of the bed, and had his nightly conversation with Marie's photograph on the bedside table.

"Why is Jonathan Dunquin here? I wish you had confided in me. You and Becky cooked up something. Becky told me she is honoring a promise to you not to explain. You always told me to trust in a higher power. For me it is easier to trust you, so I will. You must have had a very good reason for arranging this meeting. But, is his visit for him or me?

"This farm definitely has an effect on Jonathan. When he arrived, I wasn't sure that I would end up liking him. After hearing his story from you and Becky over the years, perhaps I expected to meet that high school boy, not the edgy young man that showed up. However, he has grown on me. He is a bit self-centered, but that will change quickly when he finds someone to love and share his life. There I go again being critical and judgmental. Traits of mine that I know you would have liked to change."

Zack pulled back the covers and climbed into his double bed. He spoke to the empty pillow to his side. "Reliving so many memories with Jonathan has brought an awakening to this tired old guy. If it is possible, I miss you more at this moment than ever before. Perhaps one day I'll rest my head on the pillow for my final nap. I pray I wake somewhere with you by my side."

Awakened by the striking of the clock at the foot of the stairs, consciousness came slowly to Jonathan. The glowing bedside clock read 11:01 p.m. Jonathan slid out of bed, deciding to close the door to the room and shut out the clock's strike sounds. The room was cold after the warmth of the bed. He tiptoed to the door and peered out. The night light played shadows on the walls and floor. There was a pervasive odor, like fresh flowers, he found unsettling. He froze. Someone was walking in the hall. The floor creaked with light footfalls.

"Zack? Hey, are you having trouble sleeping? Zack, are you okay?" Jonathan whispered.

The hall was quiet. Jonathan felt a chill. He retreated, pulled on his shirt, tugged on the work jeans, and scuffed barefoot into his shoes. He left the room and searched the second floor wing of the old house. The bedrooms with open doors were unoccupied. The door to one room, most likely Claire's, was locked. The next door revealed stairs that led to the attic. Jonathan switched on the light and mounted the steps.

The large room with plaster walls was warm. Light came from a lamp on an old desk, an upholstered chair beside it. Bookcases lined one wall. Framed paintings of various sizes lay propped against the other.

A blue oriental rug in the middle of the room framed the wood trunk with brass handles and hasp that sat in its center. Jonathan remembered Zack's reference to the chest of memories in the attic that passed with the house from owner to owner.

The key was in the lock. Jonathan crouched and slowly lifted the lid. He felt faint and became lightheaded as the fragrance of flowers overwhelmed him. He rocked backwards sitting heavily on the carpet. He sat cross-legged, head in hands for several minutes. When he recovered, he stared into the venerated box.

Six neatly packed cardboard correspondence containers, approximately nine by twelve inches and three inches deep comprised the first layer of what Jonathan estimated to be six layers deep. They opened like a candy box with a paper tape hinge, each held closed with a ribbon wound around two riveted wafers.

A hand lettered note on an aging show card rested on top.

Here are professions of the love of Emmett Morgan and his beloved Hope. Please keep them safely in this trunk. This is their home where the spirits of the lovers may visit.

Thank you for your kindness.
Sarah Fuller, the loving sister of Emmett Morgan."

He carefully moved the card aside and unwound the ribbon from the first box. Inside, clear plastic protectors held a sheet of age-yellowed paper.

Of course, he thought about the effort to archive the page safely, this is Marie's touch. Further examination showed that the correspondence was arranged chronologically. Jonathan read the first hand-written message.

> *My dearest Hope, we met mere days ago and since our meeting my heart has belonged to you. If souls do speak, then surely, mine has professed its deepest love and yours has heard. I dare believe that your soul has responded, for my heart bursts with joy.*
> *I am yours, Emmett.*

Jonathan trembled when he held Hope's answer.

> *Emmett, love fills my heart and my soul as well, my very being is yours. The joy of loving you fills my waking thoughts and all my dreams. Never could I have imagined that loving someone would be so grand. The moments we are apart are almost unbearable, but the promise of spending a lifetime with you consoles me.*
> *With deepest love,*
> *Hope.*

Obviously, educated people wrote the correspondence and journals in the chest. That was rare in the early nineteenth century. This made the contents even more exciting.

Jonathan reverently picked up the next sheet of yellowed correspondence. It was Emmett's response.

> *Sweet Hope, It is as though my life has started new. I rise loving the sun more each day because it also shines on you. The bouquet you gave me …*

Jonathan's eyes filled with tears and the message blurred. He put the paper down and struggled to catch his breath. Why was he

142

reacting like this?

The fragrance of flowers was stronger. Jonathan went to the box of facial tissue on the old desk. He fell into the old chair and wept.

Alone in the attic room, a myriad of visions played in Jonathan's mind, too real to be imagined, but impossible to be memories. A plain woman in a simple dress covered by an apron carefully arranged an abundant bouquet of magnificent flowers in a large delftware vase. Jonathan watched in silence. He was sitting upright in a wooden chair; there was soulful compassion on the woman's face. He looked back at the trunk filled with memories. The lid was closed. He sighed deeply and thought he heard a soft voice saying, "Enough for now."

Still wiping tears from his eyes, Jonathan returned to the guest room and lay dressed on the covers. He heard the old clock strike on the hour and on the half. He listened to the creaking of the old floors and imagined Emmett, Hope, Sarah, Rebecca, Joseph, Oakwood, and Marie walking there in life. Jonathan drifted into sleep.

Jonathan awoke and opened his eyes. He was alone in the dark guest room, the fragrance of flowers still strong. The illuminated clock read 4:15 a.m. Something was different. He switched on the bedside lamp. The drawer of the nightstand was open. It had not been earlier. As his eyes adjusted to the light, he peered inside. A small white envelope read, "Jonathan Dunquin, Personal and Confidential."

Jonathan read the enclosed message.

Chapter Twenty-One

Saturday, December 22

Zack heard the shower running as he began to prepare breakfast. The grandfather clock struck the first chime of 6:00 a.m. as Jonathan passed the large window. He noted that the snowstorm had lightened.

When Jonathan entered the warm kitchen, the smell of fresh brewed coffee was pleasingly strong, and Zack was removing hot butter biscuits from the oven.

"This will keep us warm until we can have a full farm breakfast," Zack said while directing Jonathan to the table with a nod of his head.

The two ate in silence

After breakfast, as the snow-filled sky brightened, Jonathan and Zack bundled up and headed for the barn. The sun would not be fully up for over an hour. Even then, it would be hidden behind the clouds.

In the barn, the hungry horses and excited cats greeted the men.

"With only the five horses it won't take us long. We'll feed them first, then have our breakfast, and muck the stalls later. I spoke to Ben already this morning, if he and Tim can make it they will be here to help." Zack promised.

Jonathan had hoped the other men would be there soon for mucking, it looked to him like the Percherons might dump more than four average horses. Closer inspection of the oversized stalls confirmed his fear.

Jonathan filled water buckets while Zack measured out grain and fed the cats. Once all the horses had grain, the sounds of snorting impatience gave over to the familiar sound of crunching heads and restless feet.

Zack finished before Jonathan and sat down on the bench facing the barn's wide aisle.

Jonathan approached Zack. Without explanation, he removed his gloves, reached into his jacket pocket, and handed the letter he found in the guest room to Zack.

Zack studied the handwriting on the small envelope and looked at Jonathan quizzically. He slid the single page out and held the folded sheet.

Jonathan nodded to Zack to read the message.

Still confused, slowly, Zack unfolded the page and began reading.

> Dear Jonathan,
>
> I am writing this note, knowing that my time on earth is short. By now, you know how Zack, Becky, and I have followed your life since high school. What you do not know is why it is so important for you to be here, now.
>
> Soon, you will have an opportunity to correct an error made in the past, one that caused suffering, and the denial of the happiness of others.
>
> I pray that you recognize what the Universe is offering.
> God bless you.
> Marie Todd.

Zack looked stunned. "This is Marie's handwriting. Where did you get this?" he demanded.

"Zack, did you put this letter in the guest room bed stand for me to find? Do you know anything about this?"

Zack leaned back in stunned surprise. He held the letter with one hand resting on his lap. "Honestly Jonathan, I knew nothing of this, I am as shocked as you must be."

"Can you venture a guess as to what it means?" Jonathan asked.

Zack just stared off without responding. Homer sensed the need to comfort Zack, and placed his head on the old man's knee.

Zack and Jonathan silently returned to the farmhouse. As soon as they had removed their outerwear, Homer nuzzled Zack his breakfast request.

With Homer fed, Zack poured two cups of hot coffee and brought them to the table where Jonathan was already sitting.

Zack sat heavily. "Well, this is an unexpected turn," he said. "Jonathan, you must believe that I know nothing about that letter being in the guest room. I can't imagine why no one else mentioned it. How could it have gone undetected? It must have been there since before Marie died, for over three years."

"I don't think so Zack, the table drawer was closed when I went to bed, I would have noticed it open earlier. During the night, I thought I heard something, so I left the guest room for a few minutes and went to the attic. I opened the chest and read a couple of the letters. Earlier you said that you bought the farm from the Wakefield family. Oakwood Wakefield was the second owner and you mentioned the farm being built by someone named Emmett."

Zack nodded. "The dairy farm was a successful enterprise. Oakwood Wakefield's brother inherited the dairy farm. He took over the property after the murders. The Wakefield family lived here for two generations until Marie and I bought it.

"It's obvious the notes and letters in the attic belonged to a man by the name of Emmett and a woman by the name of Hope. Did they live here or did the trunk come from somewhere else?"

Zack looked up and said, "We saw the wood chest in the attic before we purchased the farm. Tied to one handle was a pleading note asking subsequent owners never to remove it or its contents from the attic. The woman showing us the house told us it held old love letters from prior owners. The trunk transfers with the sale of the real estate. When we bought the property, we were obliged to post a bond and sign a custodial contract stating that the trunk and its contents will never leave this house.

"After we moved in, Marie and I found love letters dating back to before the house was built. The trunk also contained journals written over several years by Emmett, Hope, and Emmett's sister Sarah. Marie and I spent many hours together reading the letters and journals from that chest. I researched newspaper accounts of the time." Zack adjusted himself in the chair for comfort and began telling the story.

"The original farm was built in 1805, by Emmett Morgan. He built this house for his future bride. Emmett owned and operated a quarry down in the valley. You may have noticed that the front steps are old ships ballast stones. They came from the Morgan Quarry.

"Emmett met Hope McBride at her brother Margate's house while she was visiting from Boston. Margate was the Morgan quarry's supervisor and a close friend of Emmett's.

"Journals left in the house tell the story of the lovers. Emmett and Hope announced their engagement shortly after they met. Hope stayed with Margate and his family so she could be near Emmett and watch the building of the house.

"There is also a kind of scrapbook with the letters that Hope and Emmett had put together. Hope pressed flowers between the pages and wrote notes. She described the spring when she supervised the flower garden planting around the gazebo. There are still dried leaves and dried flowers in the book from the first blooms.

"Hope wrote a great deal about the flowers around the gazebo, the hanging vines and lilac bushes. How much she loved the fragrances, and how she enjoyed the long, bright summer days and romantic sunsets. She even wrote notes to the unborn children she expected to have with Emmett and bring up in this house.

"Some of Emmett's letters to Hope and his journals tell of his deep love for her. They are quite touching. His writing after the accident changed."

"Was the man that built this house an accident victim?" As soon as Jonathan asked the question, his heart sunk.

"I told you the original road along the top of the ridge ran near the edge. It was probably an Indian lookout post at one time. No doubt white settlers expanded the road there because it required removal of fewer trees.

"Hope traveled to Boston to have her wedding dress made. When Hope returned, Emmett picked her up at the stage station. The weather turned bad before they reached the ridge. Emmett knew he was close to home, and in a hurry to get Hope to warmth and safety. What he did not know, was that the torrential rain washed out the road. The storm rattled the horses and they probably mistook the rushing water as a stream to be crossed. They fell and slid over the cliff. Hope and the team of horses crashed to their deaths. Emmett received crippling injuries, but he survived."

Jonathan felt ill.

Zack continued, "Emmett's widowed sister, Sarah, discovered the accident scene. Her journals are also in the chest. She stayed to care for her brother until he died. Sarah wrote about her brother's depression. Emmett lived with heart-wrenching guilt. Emmett wrote in his journal that Hope was desperately frightened to be traveling in the storm. She pleaded with him to stop and wait for the storm to pass but he pushed on. He blamed himself for Hope's death."

Chapter Twenty-Two

Do We Live More Than One Life?

The two bewildered men sat quietly contemplating.

Jonathan broke the silence, "I still don't get it. What connection do you think I might have with anyone who once lived here?"

"Jonathan, I don't know."

"Do you think Becky left the note in the drawer at Marie's request, and Claire came back and opened the drawer so I would find it? Or, perhaps Claire put it there last night?" Jonathan asked, obviously agitated. "How can you be so sure your daughter didn't return last night? If she did, she could have put the note in the drawer while I was in the attic. Maybe she is in her room now."

Zack just shook his head in confusion. "None of what you suggest is at all likely. I know my daughter and granddaughter very well. They are not tricksters. If Marie asked either or both of them to deliver a letter to you, they would have been more direct. They would not have taken the chance of you finding it yourself. And, there is no way that Claire has returned to the house without me knowing.

"Ben told me this morning that the roads from the city have been impassable. Your car is in Claire's bay in the garage, there are no cars in the driveway, and my Claire would let me know if she had returned. For crying out loud, Jonathan, the woman leaves me notes when she goes to the barn."

"Zack, things have been happening to me since I arrived. Unexplainable things—some very strange," Jonathan said. "I have never hallucinated before in my life, and I have had visions, some of them have made me feel ill."

"Maybe you are coming down with the flu. I can tell you that I have done nothing to cause you to have hallucinations," Zack growled angrily.

The old man took a few moments to gain control, "It's times like this that I know Marie would have the answer. If she were still alive, she would encourage you to be open and accepting of whatever was happening to you. It was her way of dealing with everything."

Grinning, Zack said, "She might try to make you a believer. Marie had strong convictions about many things that used to strike me as odd, but she also had a number of friends and family members who shared her beliefs. Since her passing, I admit that I have started to rethink my old attitudes.

"Marie believed that the souls of people who die without completing what they were here to do have another chance at life. She said it made sense that our loving Creator would give each of us more than one chance. She would say, 'if we didn't get life right one time, we must do it over until we do.' The way Marie would talk about it with friends and our daughters, especially our granddaughter Becky, it never sounded too difficult to believe but still, I shrugged it off.

"Jonathan, I told you Marie was very intuitive. She obviously was convinced that she had a mission with some connection to you and this farm. If I were you I would not dismiss it lightly." Zack's mischievous grin returned.

"Zack, you claim that you don't buy the reincarnation theory, yet you infer that there could be something to it. Do you think I am a reincarnation of Emmett, or good God, I hope, not Oakwood or Joseph?"

Zack laughed. "I said that I didn't understand everything Marie believed about reincarnation. I have lived too long to dismiss any possibilities. Marie talked a great deal about multiple life experiences. She said we were probably together in another life. I pretended not to pay much attention, but in my heart, I found the concept comforting. Having the chance to return in a self-directed purgatory, given the opportunity to ultimately reach a spiritual union with our Creator sounds good to me. Actually, I admit that I try to believe it.

"Marie used to say that when we return we come back for the experience of resolving the unresolved. She said that the experience could be painful or a happy reward, whatever, the result was worth it. She believed that a soul could seek another soul from a past life to work out differences. If one hurts another in one life, she believed that they have to make it up to the victim in their next incarnation together.

"She also believed that a reincarnation experience was gender and race neutral unless the lessons were related to gender or race issues. As examples, she suggested that if a white man abused a man of color, in one life, he might return a man of color in the next. An abusive husband might come back as an abused wife."

"Is that a yes or a no, Zack? Do you think I am a reincarnation of someone connected with this farm?"

"Going by what I remember Marie talking about, you could be an incarnation of Emmett, Margate, Hope, Sarah, Oakwood, Rebecca, Joseph, or someone who worked on the farm. You could have been one of the poor suicidal souls who jumped from the ridge top, or a victim thrown off the cliff. You might have been the one that did the throwing—or none of these."

Now Jonathan laughed nervously, "That's not very comforting. Do you have any idea what Marie means in the letter?" He pleaded.

"None at all!" Zack responded.

Chapter Twenty-Three

Mucking Stalls is Hard Work

The phone rang while Zack and Jonathan were cleaning up their breakfast dishes. It was Ben asking Zack if he could get along without him and Tim in the barn. They were doing all they could do to keep up with necessary snow removal. Zack assured them he and Jonathan could handle the remaining morning barn chores. Upon hearing his side of the conversation, Jonathan groaned his loudest groan to which Homer answered musically.

With Zack's efficiency and directions, the chore of mucking the stalls was even more work than Jonathan had imagined. Each horse was moved to an empty stall while his or her stall was cleaned. Jonathan shoveled dung and wet cedar chips into a wheelbarrow. Jonathan grunted several heavy, steaming wheelbarrow-full loads to a snow covered manure pile behind the barn.

At one point Jonathan asked how they handled daily cleaning of many stalls, with barns full of horses. Zack told him they used a small bucket loader, but that for this few horses that would be overkill.

"Lead me to your loader," Jonathan quipped.

The comment received a closed mouth grin from Zack.

After Jonathan finished mucking a stall, Zack spread a deep blanket of fresh cedar chips on the cleaned floor. With their hoofs picked clean, each horse was returned to their refreshed compartment. All the horses received flakes of hay and fresh water. Zack and Jonathan swept the barn aisle together.

Before Jonathan could sit down, Zack headed for the door saying, "We'll come back later to brush them."

Zack and Jonathan emerged from the barn into a whiteout. The house appeared as a faint gray mass behind the blur of swirling flakes. Each man tucked his head into the raised collar of their jacket. Homer happily ran in circles, driving his snout through the fresh cold snow. Jonathan strained to see the hidden cliff. Knowing that Redemption Ridge rose, screened behind the storm, the feeling of a cold hand gripped his stomach.

Jonathan shook free of their storm wear, helped Zack dry Homer and mop the mudroom floor. Zack poured two cups of steaming black coffee and handed one to Jonathan.

Back in the library, Zack picked up the frayed copy of Nobel House and settled into his chair. It was a clear statement that they would take a break from the interviewing and any further discussion of Marie's note to Jonathan.

"That book seems to have seen a lot of wear," Jonathan commented.

"I enjoy Cavell's style of writing and the tai-pans series about the import trading competition for the period is something that I can relate to. Rereading a favorite novel is like revisiting old friends."

With Zack's permission, Jonathan built up the fire, and then browsed the exceptional stacks. He found an extensive selection of books on the subjects of world religions, spirituality, metaphysics, supernatural, and the paranormal, obviously Marie's contributions. Jonathan decided he needed some distraction and selected a 1922 first edition of Tales of the Jazz Age, short stories by F. Scott Fitzgerald, and settled down across from Zack at the opposite side of the glowing fireplace.

Zack looked over at Jonathan. "I noticed you didn't take a book from Marie's collection, are you still anxious about being chased by ghosts?"

"Not anxious, but I do find it unsettling," Jonathan squirmed in his chair. "Zack, I'm planning on leaving as soon as the roads are passable. That will probably be this evening. I can help you with the horses and barn before I go. You better call Tim and Ben so they will be available tomorrow morning."

"Suit yourself." Zack said.

Before Zack returned to his reading Jonathan asked, "What will you do by yourself before your daughter returns Monday?"

The old man chuckled. "Well, tonight I will do the same thing that Marie and I did every Saturday night that we were alone together, listen to old records in the den and read. Being alone, I'll probably do the same thing Sunday night."

"It must bring back painful memories."

"Jonathan, the memories I have of Marie are never painful. Bittersweet, yes, and they bring on some melancholy, but they also keep me close to the love of my life. I say it often, and mean it. Knowing the deep love for another is a treasured blessing."

The two men were quiet and reflective. After a few moments, each opened their books and began to read.

There was the sound of a truck in the driveway, followed by a knock on the back door. Ben had plowed again and stopped to check up on Zack.

Jonathan asked for a report on road conditions. Ben said that despite the continuing snow, the roads were becoming passable after plowing and salt treatment. He thought the interstates might be slower going than usual but it was likely that traffic would be light heading into the city in snow if Jonathan planned late night travel.

Jonathan considered this a good report and planned his departure after bedding down the horses that evening.

The two men lunched together quietly. Jonathan helped Zack clean the dishes and the kitchen, and then Zack turned the tables on Jonathan and became the interviewer. He was interested in everything. What were Jonathan's plans and dreams, how did he enjoy Wharton, working for the paper, his experiences living in the big city? Zack inquired about Jonathan's family but showed serious concern about Jonathan's lack of a love interest.

Zack stopped what he was doing to make a point. "Jonathan, I sincerely hope that you find your soul mate as I found my Marie. It is truly a blessing, to love another so completely that you are able to put your own self-interest aside."

"You think that I am self-centered?"

One corner of Zack's mouth pulled up. He shrugged, "There are indications."

Slowly the old man's wisdom penetrated Jonathan. He found that sharing his brief life experiences was exciting and brought unexpected and wonderful new insights, and an emerging self-realization. Jonathan answered Zack's questions openly with some self-criticism. Zack refused to patronize him on any of the subjects that reflected Jonathan's own perceived shortcomings. Each time Jonathan berated himself Zack asked Jonathan why he thought that he needed that experience.

Soon the two were sharing everyday life experiences and expanding on a variety of subjects. Jonathan had become less concerned about Marie's note, but the message snuck into his memory at intervals.

Jonathan listened to the old man's quiet, clear voice, straining so as not to miss a word of this magical old man's wonderful philosophy. This was really the good stuff—this was intriguing. Zack paid no attention to the tiny tape recorder's humming.

Periodically, Zack's comments would include personal experiences with Marie. As Zack shared his wonderful story about a life with a woman that he still loved very deeply Jonathan easily pictured them together as the younger Zack and the younger Marie whose photographs were displayed on the credenza in the upstairs hall.

Mid afternoon, the two men returned to the barn. Zack tuned the radio to the Saturday afternoon opera broadcast, and joked about having cultured Percherons. He said Marie's Arabians preferred light, classical music.

Each horse in turn was led to the cross ties and both men brushed the heavy winter coats.

"This is a treat for the horse," Zack offered, "my guess is that they look forward to it when they are stuck in the barn like this."

Jonathan found his fear of the giants disappeared. Brushing the equine coats clean and watching the magnificent animal's muscles shudder appreciatively under his touch gave him a feeling of peace. He enjoyed feeling the warmth they emitted. The coarse brushed hair gave off the pleasant tatami odor of rush grass.

When Zack opened Percy's stall door, he took a carrot from his pocket and handed it to Jonathan. "I think Percy feels bad about frightening you," Zack said, his eyes twinkling mischievously. "Give him this and he'll know you accept his apology."

More comfortable now, Jonathan presented the carrot in a flat hand. Percy sniffed the carrot, rubbed the side of his huge head against Jonathan's shoulder, then, using his large soft lips, he gently removed the carrot from Jonathan's hand.

Filled with the pride of his newfound friendship, Jonathan began talking softly to Percy; he led the massive animal to the crossties and began brushing the horse's neck. Zack fed carrots to the other horses while Jonathan happily finished Percy's grooming by himself.

After returning Percy to his stall, Jonathan joined Zack on the bench.

"You seem to have recovered from the shock of finding Marie's note," Zack commented.

"Some, but not fully, piecing everything together, there still are too many unanswered questions. I know that Becky told Marie about my family situation while Becky and I were still in high school. For some reason Marie thought it was important for you and I to meet, and she arranged this meeting years ago. Marie wrote a note to me before she died and somehow arranged for me to find it in your guest room nightstand drawer. What I cannot figure out is why Marie found me important in the first place. How could she have planned my visit years ago? How would she have known I would be trapped by a storm and spend the night in your guest room? How did the drawer open during the night? There's the note itself, what does it mean? And there are the visions—are they coincidental? Am I coming down with something?"

Before Jonathan could curb his tongue, the words were out, "Are you drugging me?"

A shocked look crossed Zack's face. "Jonathan, don't go thinking that way. I understand your confusion, but I can't help you, we are both in the dark here. Let's go back to the house and relax with a glass of wine before dinner. After dinner, you can rest before you head home."

Jonathan had slipped back into a dark mood, but he had no choice but to return to the house and try to control his emotions. He was prepared to sulk and not eat, but the temptation was too great, and before an hour had passed he found himself drawn to the kitchen, enjoying another of Zack's meals.

Saturday night dinner was Coq au Vin (Vin Jaune, Cream Morels) over egg noodles. Zack shared his secret that blanching the bacon before cooking reduces the saltiness. He served the same wine that he cooked the dish with, saying, "Do not cook with a wine you would not drink."

After dinner, contented and relaxed, the two men went to a room Jonathan had not been in before. More formal than the library, a petite grand piano was the focal point. Matching wing back chairs flanked the fireplace, each with its own reading lamp and side table. A large credenza of polished mahogany housed a record turntable, stereo amplifier, and a boxlike vertical storage of long play albums library. Zack opened the unit's doors and uncovered internal speakers.

Zack waved Jonathan to a chair. "You asked what I do Saturday nights. I select a mix of jazz and swing going back over forty years. Let's see, right in front we have Jonah Jones, Ella Fitzgerald, Billie Holiday, Erroll Garner, Julie London, some Frank Sinatra, and a favorite of mine, Dakota Staton. Let's start with Ella."

The music played at a comfortable conversational level, and Zack commented about the events in his life with Marie and memories triggered by each piece. Jonathan began enjoying the memory lane concert. He felt ashamed of his earlier paranoid suspicions. He began to recognize the deep feelings he had developed for Zack and the very special woman, Marie, who was so alive in Zack's memory.

Around 9:30, Zack drifted off. Jonathan quietly went upstairs to the guest room to change from the loaned farm clothing into his own for the drive home. Before changing, he sat on the bed and replayed the past several hours in his mind.

Although he had planned to leave, something was holding him, an elusive thought tugged on the periphery of his conscious mind. He turned and stared at the still open drawer where he found Marie's note. Then he removed the note from his shirt pocket and read it again. Lying back on the bed with the note on his chest Jonathan was the most comfortable that he had been since arriving.

"You are here to learn." The sound of his own voice startled him. Jonathan bolted upright. There was no vision, no mysterious fragrance. At that moment, he knew that he would not leave that night. He had to stay at the farm.

When Jonathan went downstairs, he found Zack still asleep and the record player stopped. He gently nudged Zack awake. "Zack, it's time for bed."

Zack stretched, when he was fully awake he asked, "Are you leaving?"

"No, if it's alright with you I'll stay another night."

"It's better than alright. I'm happy to hear that."

A drowsy Homer followed both men to the kitchen. Jonathan assumed Zack's task and went to the mudroom, letting Homer out. The dog was back in seconds. Homer licked Jonathan's face during the towel drying and went back to the kitchen for a drink. Jonathan followed, laughing at Homer's loud lapping. He turned to see Zack looking at the barn monitor with a concerned expression. Zack rushed to the mudroom and pulled on his boots and jacket. "Something is wrong," he shouted to Jonathan.

Chapter Twenty-Four

Trouble in the Barn

Jonathan yanked on the work jacket and scuffed into his boots, following Zack and the now alert Homer into the snowy night. He did not remember opening the barn door but he was the first inside, searching for the light switch. Zack was close behind and quickly filled the barn with overhead light. Sleepy eyed horses poked heads over the opened Dutch doors of the stalls, all except one.

Zack rushed to the stall door and threw it open. Inside, the big gray Percheron mare lay on her side in obvious distress.

"We have to get her up," Zack commanded.

Jonathan joined Zack in the task of coaxing, pushing, and cajoling the massive animal onto all fours. He led the pregnant stumbling horse into the barn's wide aisle. "Keep her walking," Zack instructed Jonathan in a quiet confident tone and handed off the haltered head. "Her name is Daisy."

Zack disappeared, returning quickly with a braided leather lead hung over his shoulder. He carried a clear plastic bag containing a white liquid in one hand, and a plastic-tube turkey baster in the other. He nodded to the lead and Jonathan instinctively

159

snapped the end to Daisy's halter.

"She's too tall for me to reach, you'll have to force feed her this." Zack squeezed the bulb, filling the big tube and handed it to Jonathan. Do you know how to open her mouth?"

Jonathan's head snapped affirmatively and he performed the process he learned at the riding stable for inserting a bit.

The mare shied from the instrument and Zack pulled down hard on the braided lead lowering the big head. "Stick your thumb into her jowl and squeeze the liquid into her throat. When you do she'll toss her head, we will both have to hold her head up until she swallows it all," Zack directed.

Without thought or question, Jonathan complied. The big horse resisted, lifting Zack momentarily off his feet but the wiry old man kept the mare's head low enough for Jonathan to pour in the milky white medication. They both coaxed her to swallow with gentle words and stroking hands.

Zack's voice was calm and steady with the clarity Jonathan had grown to appreciate. "Keep her moving, keep her moving," he almost whispered. The two men repeated the procedure until the bag was empty, Zack walked beside Daisy, rubbing the horse's neck soothingly as Jonathan continued to walk her back and forth in the long aisle.

"Now we walk her until she has a good bowel movement," Zack said.

"What just happened?" Jonathan asked.

"She's colicky, I saw her down on the monitor. Colic can kill a horse. We just gave her a massive physic. That should do the trick. My worry now is that she will go into labor in which case we could lose her. We have to keep her walking until her intestines straighten out. I called the vet from the office phone, but we can't count on him coming given the storm conditions. He lives too far away."

Zack looked pitifully small beside the huge horse. "Jonathan, I don't know why you decided to stay, but I'm glad you did. I could not have handled this without your help."

Jonathan heard a noise above him. Growltiger and Etcetera lay side by side, their front paws hanging over the edge of the hayloft, watching the heroic activity below.

The two men took turns walking the mare for nearly three hours. When Jonathan walked Daisy, he called her by name, rubbed her broad nose and neck, and chatted about the baby she soon would bring into the world.

Just before 2:00 a.m., Daisy's straightened intestines allowed her to relieve herself generously on the barn floor. The two men joyfully congratulated Daisy on her fine dump and walked her until it was obvious that she was out of danger.

Jonathan could not believe that he was actually happy to be cleaning up a smelly pile of horse manure in the middle of the night. When he finished he joined Zack on the antique bench.

"What is it about horses?" Jonathan asked. "They are like big babies."

"They are that, and they need our help on occasion, but we owe the animal a great deal. Man has benefited more from the horse than we can ever repay. The horse deserves respect and pampering. Think about it. The horse has served man for centuries; man still depends on the horse for transportation, labor, and in some cultures, food. It is hard to believe that in this country, healthy horses are slaughtered for no other reason that they are too costly to keep! They deserve more respect."

Returning to the guest room, Jonathan was too tired to shower so he dragged off his clothes and crawled into bed. He planned to take a two-hour nap, then revisit the attic and the chest of memories.

Chapter Twenty-Five

Sunday December 23, 1990

Jonathan woke, shocked by the brightness of his room. It was 7:30 a.m. He swung his legs out of bed and groaned. Muscles unaccustomed to the exercise of the previous day and exhausting night complained bitterly. Jonathan stumbled to the bathroom and turned on the shower. When the shower stall filled with steam, he stepped in and let the heat penetrate his aching body.

The enticing smell of bacon frying wafted from downstairs, Jonathan skipped shaving, put on fresh work clothes and went to the kitchen.

Zack was at the vintage range turning a puffy omelet onto a plate. He was all smiles when he set it at Jonathan's regular place at the table, "Sit down Jonathan and get this while it's hot. I have already been in the barn and Daisy is doing fine. She said to thank you, again."

"This looks too good to eat," Jonathan commented, then sliced off a large portion with his fork. Zack looked on appreciatively as Jonathan enjoyed the most recent culinary creation. When he finished the last bite of crisp bacon, Jonathan said,

"Zack, despite everything that has upset me here, I am really glad I came. Meeting you has been a very special experience. To begin with, you are not the man I expected to interview. You are far more, and much better. When I arrived, this farm scared me. The horses scared me. The crazy visions scared me. Now, I feel as though I have become a different person in just the past few hours."

A knowing expression crossed Zack's heavily creased face.

After breakfast Jonathan, Zack, and Homer went to the barn to see to their charges. Jonathan immediately went to Daisy and hugged the big head. Zack measured grain and Jonathan cleaned and refilled water buckets.

Jonathan climbed into the old loft and tossed the hay bales to the barn floor while Zack sat on the handmade bench, watching with quiet delight.

Snow was lighter and the outline of the ridge had become visible when the two men and dog headed back to the house.

Zack and Jonathan cleaned their hands at the kitchen sink and Zack invited Jonathan to assist in preparation of their lunch. He offered Jonathan a traditional French aperitif of strong Pastis as a toast to their success in bringing Daisy back to good health.

Lunch was from Zack's Sub Zero freezer. He produced a container of hearty homemade pea soup and partially baked imported French baguettes. Jonathan heated the soup while Zack set the table and poured a Pinot Noir for each of them. The baguettes finished baking in a 350-degree oven. They filled the air with the smell of fresh bread. The steaming soup teemed with chunks of ham and cooked carrots. Zack dropped a dollop of sour cream on each serving. It was a simple meal but Jonathan could not remember a lunch that he enjoyed more. He capped each piece of bread with Brie and savored the blend of flavors. Zack's special blend of black coffee was sufficient dessert.

Light classical music aided the choreographed Sunday afternoon barn activity. Zack said the tape was a favorite in the Arabian horse barn when Marie was alive. The Percherons seemed equally appreciative.

Jonathan found brushing the gentle animals satisfying. Neither he nor Zack spoke, each absorbed in his own thoughts.

The storm had lightened and the outline of Resurrection Ridge was a distant shadow as the two men returned wearily to the farmhouse. Only Homer seemed to be enjoying the fresh snow. The old dog delighted in scooping snow with his nose into a pile on his snout then shaking it off.

"I don't know about you, my young friend, but this old man needs a nap after our late night in the barn."

"Sounds very good to me," Jonathan responded as they entered the warm house.

They each retired to their rooms. Both men were asleep in a matter of a few minutes.

At 6:00 p.m., their internal clocks in harmony, Zack and Jonathan rendezvoused in the kitchen. They dined on grilled bratwurst, sauerkraut, baked beans, and brown bread, washed down with a dark German beer.

After cleaning the kitchen, the two spent a couple of hours in the barn talking to each horse, petting them, and preparing them for the night. When it was time to leave Jonathan's heart was heavy as he slid the door closed to the dimly lighted barn.

It was nearly midnight when Jonathan prepared to leave, hoping the late hour would mean lighter traffic and better driving conditions.

With the farm's long driveway plowed, Jonathan stood in the back doorway of the now familiar farmhouse facing his host. The sound of the car's engine idled, overpowered by the whirling sound of its heater fan. The windshield wipers beat slowly against the lightly falling snow.

Jonathan could not resist the temptation to give the extraordinary man before him a big hug.

"Zack, I can't tell you what this visit with you has meant to me," Jonathan choked, "you are truly an extraordinary man."

Zack's deep, clear eyes fixed on Jonathan, "When anyone said anything like that to Marie she would tell them they were seeing a reflection of themselves."

In an attempt to ease the separation, Zack added jovially, "You'll find my favorite snow shovel on the floor in the back seat of your car along with a bucket of sand, just in case you need it! Remember, I want both the shovel and the bucket back. You can do whatever with the sand."

As he started to slide into the driver's seat, Jonathan exuberantly shouted, "You bet I'll be back!"

"Good," Zack said quietly, "and bring that beautiful new lady of yours with you."

"If I ever find her," Jonathan scoffed.

"You will," Zack said with certainty. "You will, I have a suspicion that is what Marie meant in her note."

Jonathan went back to Zack. A bit uneasy, he asked, "Zack, before I leave I just have to ask who is the woman? I have felt her presence several times in the house. Please tell me, is it Marie's spirit?"

Zack stood expressionless for several long seconds. Jonathan sat down on the boot box beside the door, a firm statement that he meant to wait for an answer. Outside the opened door, the car's wipers thumped their tuneless rhythm.

Zack sat down next to Jonathan, "No Jonathan, I don't think Marie is here in any form other than in my memory. I don't doubt that you experienced something, and I think whatever it is will serve you well. If you have had contact with another level of consciousness, I think it is loving, but not Marie.

"Let me tell you a story. Shortly after Marie and I moved into this house, I was driving home at dusk when I came upon a woman walking in the lane. It was at the turn under the ridge. I stopped, and asked if she was going to the farm and she nodded. It was just before Christmas, snowing lightly and already accumulating on the road. The road wasn't paved then and walking was bound to be difficult. I offered her a ride and she refused, shaking her head. I couldn't blame her for not getting into a car with a strange man. She was dressed for the weather with a long hooded cape and the farm wasn't far so I drove on.

"Marie met me at the door. I told her about the woman and asked if she knew who she was. Marie was annoyed that I didn't insist on her getting in the car. Marie grabbed a jacket and we went all the way to the base of the ridge. The woman wasn't there. I got out of the car and walked back up the road a bit to see if she had gone off into the meadow. Then, I noticed my footprints were the only ones in the new snow."

"Are you telling me that you met a woman's spirit on the lane?"

"I'm telling you about an experience that is difficult to explain. Perhaps like the experiences you say you have had here," Zack said quietly.

"So, you admit now that there is a possibility of departed spirits returning in some human form."

"If I were to speculate, I might admit that there could be a force that makes us believe we have seen something supernatural. Marie lived a very spiritual life; she saw things that others didn't see and had a knowing. She often talked about an afterlife that differed from most fundamental religion's concepts. She enjoyed discussions and often referenced what she believed to be credible information, even credible speculation. Metaphysical philosophy and the supernatural intrigued her.

"I try to believe what Marie believed. Marie's belief kept her positive and happy. She did not fear death. She said that she prepared before her death to spend a long time in terms of our life years in soulful reflection. She said that she knew that her soul had to be ready if it was to advance, or return to another mortal experience, or any experience at any level of growth."

Zack stood, the outside noise faded as he closed the door.

"I have lived long enough to experience things that I don't understand." Zack sat next to Jonathan again. "Sometimes it is difficult, but it is wise to keep your mind open to possibilities. Paranormal concepts are difficult to believe, but before television I never would have thought that images of live people could be sent through the air. Many things we take for granted today were considered sorcery once. Can you imagine telling a nineteenth-century doctor that twentieth-century medicine would be able to transplant a human heart?"

Zack continued, "Before her death Marie felt directed to bring you here for this visit? I can't say why or how, but obviously she was able to arrange our meeting in an extraordinary way."

Jonathan was uncomfortable and sputtered, "I still don't understand any of this."

Zack studied Jonathan.

"My young friend," he said sternly, "you still have a great deal to learn—but, you will learn!" Without looking up, he cleared his throat, "Something very special has happened to you here, and I'm happy for you. Keep your mind open to new possibilities, and remember that we are all part of a grand design. Marie taught me to be open even if I could not be a committed believer. She would say, 'Remember that not everything that happens to us or because of us is intended directly to affect only us. We are not here alone. Perhaps our only true purpose in being here is to open a door one day so that another may pass through.'

"Now, it's important that you get back to New York City, so get going. You have a great life ahead!"

"I'll return your shovel," Jonathan said and hugged the old man again at the open doorway. He did the leather sole shuffle on slippery snow to his car. When he looked back, Jonathan shrugged and Zack grinned widely.

Zack looked so small standing there in the doorway as Jonathan waved a final goodbye from the driveway.

Chapter Twenty~Six

Back to the City

Over the slick back roads to the highway, Jonathan thought about the three days and the strange experiences. His thoughts led only to more questions. He cautiously identified his direction and entered the interstate; just behind a brigade of snowplows driving abreast. He dared not get too close, benefiting from the freshly cleared path. He kept the truck's flashing lights in view while driving into a swirling white tunnel.

This is symbolic, Jonathan thought. Zack would love it. Here I am in the worst snowstorm to hit the northeast in years and I have my own battalion of snowplows to clear my path.

The hours passed. Jonathan thought about the years of extraordinary love Zack and Marie shared. His thoughts turned to his own family. How his parents dealt with their child's illness and death. How bravely his young sister faced her suffering.

This brought his thoughts back to Zacharie and Marie Todd and their unselfish generosity. He compared his twenty-nine years of relative insulation from major problems. His graduate degree prepared him for a rewarding career, but did not compare to the accumulated wisdom of a ninth-grade-educated man and his decades of experience.

In the distance, Jonathan could see a brightening and a slit of color on the horizon. The sun was rising and snowflakes were getting bigger. The blacktop was showing on the road for the first time in over one-hundred miles. One by one, the snowplows pulled off the highway until Jonathan's was one of very few cars on a cleared wet pavement.

The storm stopped completely by the time that Jonathan entered the city. Parked cars, hydrants, partially buried bicycles, even the trashcan lids glistened with the fresh snow covering. That would not last long Jonathan thought, but how good it made him feel to see it that way.

Reflecting on his time with Zack made the trip pass quickly. Jonathan was surprised, he should have been exhausted but he wasn't. The quiet city seemed like it was there just for him.

Back in his modest apartment, Jonathan found Sue's message rescheduling the dinner party for Christmas Eve. It was the only one on his answering machine. Jonathan was delighted; he had no other plans for Christmas Eve.

Jonathan scrambled some eggs and made coffee. Neither matched Zack's culinary touch. Then he went to bed and tried to make up for the hours of lost sleep.

The phone woke Jonathan just after 2:00 p.m. Monday afternoon. It was Sue.

"Good, you are home. I cannot wait to hear all about your adventure. Was the storm terrible in the mountains?" Sue enthusiastically gushed.

"The Berkshires are hardly mountains, and yes there was a lot of snow. What about Christmas Eve, your other friends, are they still on for dinner at your place?" Jonathan asked hopefully.

"Oh they will be. You'll like them I'm sure," Sue said.

Jonathan was excited and apprehensive. Shades of Priscilla and the handsome riding instructor returned, and he began to feel depressed.

The rest of Monday and all day Tuesday dragged by, Jonathan worked on the Zack Todd story. It was hard to stay focused, reliving the visit to Todd's farm. He found himself trying to imagine what Zack was doing in the old house.

Chapter Twenty-Seven

Christmas Eve

Snow flurries caused Jonathan to check the weather channel periodically. He feared that dinner plans would be canceled again.

Jonathan was excited and burned off excess energy with a long midday walk. It was fun watching the last minute Christmas shoppers scurrying about. He took an excessive amount of time at the package store selecting wine for his hosts, finally settling for their well-known favorite.

At 5:00 p.m., Jonathan showered, shaved, and dressed. He changed clothes three times. Finally satisfied he examined himself closely in the mirror to be certain the last hair was in place. His reflection glowed back with a smile of artificial self-approval, reminding him of a baby with gas.

At 6:30, he pulled on his own properly fitting galoshes. They reminded him of the clumsy overshoes, the barn, New England, and Zack. What was he doing now? Was he in the barn with the sweet smell of hay and horses, or was he in the warm country kitchen creating at his magnificent stove? Jonathan could feel the broad grin on his face as he looped the once forgotten natty scarf around his neck and donned his warm camel hair top coat.

Jonathan stretched an expensive calfskin glove over his left hand and slapped the right glove into the palm. With the holiday-wrapped box containing his friend's wine snugly tucked under his arm Jonathan locked up, stepped sprightly into the elevator, and descended to the street below.

Deciding walking would be easier than driving and finding a parking place, Jonathan breathed in the cold air and strode light-heartedly along.

Life was great. Jonathan had the Todd interview, it was Christmas Eve, and he was looking forward to an exciting evening. Fine white snow started falling again and coating the sidewalk. Jonathan kicked it up playfully into powdery clouds.

Jeff and Sue had a great home. Although a modest building, the former owner expanded into an adjacent apartment, completely renovated, and professionally decorated. Sue and Jeff decided to forego the services of a door-manned building in exchange for a view and square footage. French doors from the living room led to a balcony with a fabulous skyline view.

At the front entry of the building, Jonathan skipped up the snowy steps to the door. A woman was leaving. She was bundled in a long, hooded cape. Jonathan held the door for her while she passed.

"Good evening, happy holidays." Jonathan said.

She nodded and said, "Thank you Jonathan and Merry Christmas to you." Her voice muffled behind a scarf.

Jonathan continued to hold the door in puzzlement. She called him by name. Jonathan turned to see who she was. Looking both ways and across the deserted street Jonathan was surprised she had gotten out of sight so quickly. He shrugged it off and almost ran through the lobby to the elevator.

Jeff grabbed the packaged wine from Jonathan at his apartment door with a knowing nod, threw Jonathan's coat over his arm, and commented cheerily about his scarf.

Sue descended on Jonathan gushing Merry Christmas, hugged him and smacked a big kiss on his cold cheek. She clung to

Jonathan and dragged him to the dining room to inspect the table setting. Sue had set out her finest china and crystal. Jeff pressed a bottle of beer into Jonathan's hand.

Sue winced, "Jeff, get Jonathan a glass. What am I going to do with this man, Jonathan; will he ever have any class?"

"Leave him and marry me," Jonathan joked.

The three knew each other well. Sue, Jeff, and Jonathan went to high school together. They renewed their friendship in New York when Jeff and Sue moved to the city a few months earlier. Sue transferred to the home office of an international hotel chain, and Jeff found a position bucking for a partnership in a large law firm.

This evening, the apartment smelled wonderful of the mixed cooking fragrances of baking Cornish hens and wild rice, asparagus, and hollandaise. All familiar since this was the meal that Sue always served at her dinner parties, it was fine with Jonathan, she did it well and he enjoyed it!

Jeff and Sue excused themselves and Jonathan walked toward the French doors. The telephone rang and Jeff buzzed their guests in, butterflies fluttered in Jonathan's stomach as he gazed at the lights of the city. The snow had stopped and the air was clear.

Jonathan's mind floated back to the New England farm. He envisioned Zack and Marie, the vibrant couple they must have been together, when Marie was alive. He thought about Emmett, Morgan, and Hope McBride. What would their lives have been like if Emmett had not been so willful and heeded Hope's caution? Would they have lived as long and as happy together as Zack and Marie? Jonathan knew that all that he had learned during his time with Zack had not fully processed, but it would. He knew that he was a better person for the meeting with Zack and the experience.

Sue originally arranged this dinner party so Jonathan could meet her new friend and the friend's daughter. The older woman needed a professional writer's assistance to finish her husband's memoirs. That was Sue's excuse for bringing them together, but Sue, the matchmaker, obviously was interested in having Jonathan meet the woman's twenty-something single daughter.

Sue slid up from behind and whispered in Jonathan's ear, "Martha Scott is the mother; her daughter's name is pronounced Ah-Shee-ah."

Without turning, Jonathan heard Sue rush off to join Jeff at the apartment door. There was a volley of brightly intertwined greetings and introduction to the younger visitor.

Mustering up his composure and trying to look very cool, Jonathan turned in time to meet the small group crossing the living room. Time stopped as the group seemed to float slowly in space. All three of the women were dressed beautifully and stylishly coiffured, but Ashia was astonishing. Jonathan's heart skipped a beat.

Sue arrived first and threw her arms around Jonathan at the same time turning toward her two guests, she announced, "This is Jonathan, the future Pulitzer winner! Jonathan, meet Martha Scott and Ashia."

Sue clearly pronounced the young woman's name again for Jonathan's benefit. It was unnecessary, Ashia had made an indelible impression.

Ashia cocked her head and flashed a broad smile. She was magic, a vision.

Zack's words rang in Jonathan's ears as he described his first feelings after meeting Marie. "This is the woman that I will marry, my heart leaped with joy."

Jonathan repeated Zack's words to himself, "This is the woman I will marry!"

"Jonathan, it's a pleasure to meet you," Ashia said softly as she offered her hand.

"Ashia," Jonathan heard himself say, the sound was musical.

Sue noticed the immediate chemistry between them and grinned widely.

The stately, silver-haired woman stepped forward with outstretched hand.

"Mrs. Scott," Jonathan said with a slight bow.

"Jonathan, please call me Martha," her voice was deep and mellow accompanied by a firm handshake. "Sue has told us so much about you. Ashia and I have been looking forward to our meeting. We understand the blizzard trapped you out of town. That must be an interesting story."

They talked about the heavy snowstorm that had just passed, and Jonathan related his drive back from New England as Jeff passed drinks to his new guests.

Sue watched Ashia and Jonathan with unconcealed delight. "Martha, Jeffrey and I have something in the den, you must see!"

In a flurry of excited chatter, Martha, Sue and Jeff were off, leaving Ashia and Jonathan alone in front of the French doors.

"Jonathan, it's stopped snowing, let's step out onto the balcony," Ashia said.

"It will be very cold for you."

"Just for a moment, the air will feel good." She twisted the handle, glided through the opening and across the damp deck to the rail. The glow of the interior lights seemed to follow her.

Testing the door to be certain it was unlocked, Jonathan closed it gently and stood for a moment watching Ashia. She wore her golden hair short. It swept up on the sides and back exposing an elegant neck.

"The city looks so bright and clean from here," she said, then looked up. Distant stars were twinkling between the breaking clouds.

Moving forward Jonathan removed his wool sport coat and placed it gently over Ashia's shoulders. His heart swelled. Ashia accepted his coat without turning and crossed her hands over her chest to hold it in place. Jonathan left his hands resting softly on her shoulders.

"Jonathan."

His heart fluttered.

"When Sue told me we would be meeting I looked up your name. I find etymology very interesting. Are you aware that Jonathan means Gift of God?"

"Yes, my mother lost two children before I was born and thought she was being punished for some reason, so when I came along she felt forgiven. Does that sound crazy?"

"Not at all—Dunquin, is your family Irish?"

"Yes, grandfather on my father's side, the rest of the family are all mongrels."

"What about you, Ashia?" Jonathan asked quietly. "Your name sounds middle eastern."

"It is an ancient Sanskrit. Ashia was my father's mother's name, she was Persian."

"You don't look Persian or Iranian."

She tilted her head back to Jonathan, "I was adopted. My father loved his grandmother and her name."

"Ashia. What is the Sanskrit meaning?" Jonathan asked.

"It means life and hope."

Hope. A new life, Jonathan thought.

The cold breeze stirred the familiar fragrance to him.

Chapter Twenty-Eight

Christmas Day

Already Christmas morning, and nearly 2:00 a.m. when Jonathan practically floated up the front steps to his apartment. He enthusiastically accepted sharing a cab with Mrs. Scott and Ashia. Before parting, Mrs. Scott gave Jonathan her card and suggested that he call after the holidays.

In restless sleep, Jonathan was an observer in his own dream. Emmett sat in his wooden wheel chair at the foot of the stairs in the front hall of the farmhouse. He was impatiently waiting for his sister, Sarah, to bring a packet of Hope's love letters from her guarded hideaway. Jonathan knew that Sarah carefully chose the letters she shared with her brother, to nurture the love, and lessen his depression.

The dream scene shifted to Marie, at her desk in her alcove, reading Sarah's journals. He knew that Marie shared Sarah's belief that Emmett and Hope would be united one day, but how could that be?

Church bells woke Jonathan at 7:00 a.m. on Christmas morning. At first, he was startled. He could not remember hearing them before. Jonathan literally bounded out of bed to face the bright new day. The view from his window was different. In the past, he hardly noticed the stone church on the corner. The street was alive with activity, cabs dropping off happy parties, couples walking arm in arm, families with children bouncing excitedly, all moved briskly to the church steps greeting each other along the way. Jonathan grinned appreciatively.

At the telephone, Jonathan dialed long distance, then checked the clock. He shrugged and grinned, "Hi Mom," he said cheerily, "Merry Christmas, did I wake you?" The welcomed call soon had both his Mom and Dad chattering on the line with him.

Jonathan wandered around the apartment in his underwear, twisting in and out of the old telephone's long cord. He spewed details of his Christmas Eve and the wonderful girl he had met. He spelled and repeated Ashia's name and the story of her adoption several times. "In ancient Sanskrit, Ashia means Hope. This sounds crazy, I know that I have only known her for a few hours but it seems like I have always known her all of my life. Mom, Dad, this is the woman I will marry!"

Before hanging up, Jonathan promised his parents he would visit soon and shared his intention to bring Ashia with him.

It never dawned upon Jonathan that Ashia might not share his feelings.

While singing *Winter Wonderland* in the shower, Jonathan decided to go to church. He was not Catholic, but he did not think it would matter to anyone on Christmas Day.

Jonathan dressed and arrived at the church on the corner in time for the high mass. He found the sanctuary packed with the happiest crowd he had seen together in a long time. The choir voices echoed off the vaulted ceiling. For a moment, Jonathan thought he saw a golden cloud around everyone, but when he blinked, it disappeared.

Jonathan's family brought him up as a Methodist. After arriving at college, he drifted from regular church attendance. It was not that he stopped believing, it was more that a church wasn't necessary for him to communicate with his God, he could do that any time, any place. Now, surrounded by hundreds of joyful celebrants, he understood the magic, the mystery within the sacred walls. From Bible study in his youth, Jonathan recalled; "Matthew 18:20—'for where two or three are gathered in my name, there am I [God] among them.'"

When the mass ended, Jonathan shuffled out with the throng, sharing greetings. Back in his apartment he was about to call Sue when the telephone rang. The voice on the other end of the line made his heart skip a beat.

"Merry Christmas, Jonathan, this is Ashia. Did I wake you?"

"No, in fact I have already been to church. Merry Christmas. What a pleasant surprise."

"Jonathan, mother and I enjoyed meeting you last night. I called Sue this morning and she said that you do not have any family in the area and would probably be alone today. We have friends that have reservations later at Tavern on the Green, I have never seen it at Christmas, but I'm told it is very special. We called and they can squeeze another chair at our table, will you join us as our guest?"

Heart thumping, Jonathan responded affirmatively, so happily that his voice cracked. He would meet them at the famous restaurant in Central Park. Forget about Priscilla.

When Jonathan got off the telephone it rang again, almost immediately.

"Hi Jonathan, Merry Christmas, this is Becky Baron. I'm here at the farm, Pépère Zack has been telling me about your extraordinary visit." I know that you are aware of my involvement.

"Hello Becky, I am happy to hear from you. Merry Christmas."

"I called Sue this morning to get your telephone number. She said you had an eventful Christmas Eve, that you met someone that could turn out to be very special in your life. Actually, Sue said she saw sparks flying between you and the young lady."

"Sue." Sue was Becky's connection. It all made sense now to Jonathan. Becky, Sue, and Jeff all went to the same high school with Jonathan. Sue knew all about Jonathan's family, his sister, and his activities after high school and college.

Becky's voice was steady, self-assured, "Jonathan, before you start asking me questions that I can't answer let me tell you that I have been doing what Mémère Marie asked me to do, nothing else. I don't know what motivated my grandmother, her interest in you, or why she so specifically wanted her directions followed to the letter. I loved her and respected her wishes. As far as the note to you that you found in the guest room here, my aunt Claire and I don't know anything about that. We would like to see it sometime. Pépère Zack has no doubt that my grandmother wrote it."

"I believe you. I was upset during my visit with your grandfather, so many strange things occurred. Today, I am on cloud nine, none of it matters."

Becky laughed and handed the telephone to Zack. The familiar clarity of the old man's voice warmed Jonathan's heart. They exchanged holiday greetings and Jonathan told Zack about his drive home. He described how the snowplows led his way safely to the city. The two men laughed together and Jonathan promised to call the farm on New Year's Day with an update on his new romantic interest. Jonathan's last words to Zack were, "Zack, I have met the woman I will marry."

Zack replied, "I know," and hung up the phone.

Just after the New Year, the Dunquins lovingly welcomed Ashia into their home. During the weekend visit, Jonathan and Ashia told the parents of their intentions, and that they had set a date for their wedding.

Chapter Twenty-Nine

April 1991

On a warm Sunday afternoon, Ashia and Jonathan returned Zack's shovel. Zack greeted Jonathan and his bride-to-be with twinkling eyes and his familiar knowing grin. He introduced Jonathan and Ashia to his live-in daughter Claire who invited them to stay for dinner. Claire suggested the couple to wait in the garden while she and Zack went to the house to prepare.

The antique hand-made bench from the barn was back in the gazebo. There was a moment of anticipation when Jonathan feared that the familiarity of the farm might again kindle visions, but they never recurred.

As the sun began to set, the lovers sat together, absorbed in views of grazing horses, rolling meadows, and the distant valley. With Ashia nestled in Jonathan's arms, he shared with her the details of his snowbound visit with Zack four months before. He told her about his extraordinary experiences. Ashia unquestioningly accepted Jonathan's accounts of the events.

"Jonathan, I believe there are unseen forces at work around us. You know, there is something about this place. Something that seems very familiar to me," Ashia murmured. "I feel like I have been here before."

With the fragrances of the flowers surrounding them, the young lovers witnessed the last crimson glow of the day reflected off Redemption Ridge together.

Chapter Thirty

Zack Joins Marie

few weeks after Ashia and Jonathan visited Zack on that special spring day Zack joined his beloved Marie. It saddened Jonathan, knowing he would not be able to see and talk to Zack again.

Ashia and Jonathan went to Zack's funeral and met all his surviving children, grandchildren, and great grandchildren. He introduced Ashia to Midge. They visited for a few minutes with the server from the restaurant in town and met her husband, Jake.

Midge seemed extraordinarily pleased to see Jonathan and to meet Ashia. Jonathan felt the special connection with Midge that he experienced at their first meeting, months earlier. As she turned to leave, Midge tossed a crafty look at Jonathan and shifted her gaze to Becky, who was standing with her fiancé. She turned back to Jonathan with a knowing nod of her head.

The Todd family invited the couple back to the farm. Ashia and Jonathan sat in the gazebo again and could not help but wonder if Emmett and Hope were being given another chance. They spoke of their future and plans, and agreed that they would name their first son, Zachary, and their first daughter, Marie.

Driving home from Zack's funeral with Ashia by his side, Jonathan's thoughts wandered back to Christmas Eve, 1990, the special night he met Ashia. He recalled the puzzling feeling that struck him when the woman passed at the entrance to Sue and Jeff's apartment building. How did she know his name? Thinking about it, he really wasn't sure if she had said Jonathan, or Emmett. It was only a couple of seconds before Jonathan turned to see who she was and she was gone.

At the time, Jonathan's head was filled with distracting thoughts and anticipation of the evening. More clear-headed, he remembered looking down the stairs at the sidewalk. It occurred to him. His were the only set of footprints in the fresh snow.

Since his visit with Zack, that special weekend, Jonathan had spent many hours studying and contemplating the possibility of reincarnation. He is researching claims of supernatural intercession and assistance from the other side.

Jonathan feels that Marie and Sarah used a willing Becky to bring Emmett and Hope together again. Now, Sarah and Marie, the loving matchmakers from another time, can rest in peace.

Jonathan and Ashia married that June in the vine-covered white gazebo on the Redemption Ridge Farm surrounded by a riot of color in the bloom-filled garden. Percy, the big black stallion, his summer coat brushed to sheen, witnessed the ceremony from behind the meadow fence. Across the meadow, in another pasture, Daisy, the gray mare grazed with a six-month-old black colt by her side.

Zack's daughter, Claire, and granddaughter Becky, joined Ashia and Jonathan's family and friends that exceptionally glorious day.

Becky joined the family business and moved into the Todd apartment in Manhattan. She was responsible for arranging the wedding at the farm. Her fiancé, Rev. Joseph Meier, graciously accepted to perform the ceremony.

At the end of the glorious wedding day, Becky took Jonathan aside. "I have something to show you."

"Mémère Marie gave it to me years ago, before she died. She

made me promise not to open it until a specific date." Becky turned the envelope to display the instructions written on its face.

"I carried this note with me, everywhere."

The date on the envelope passed several weeks earlier. Jonathan looked at Becky questioningly.

"Go ahead and open it."

Her grandmother's exquisite handwriting had become shaky but still identifiable.

Dearest Becky,

Your reward for serving destiny will come in the form of a question. Follow your heart.

Lovingly, Mémère Marie

He handed that note back to Becky, his face beaming with anticipation.

Becky quickly related her story, "I happened to be in New York City on business the day the note was to be opened. It was hectic and I forgot about it. That evening I joined a group of friends for dinner. A handsome and exciting man that I hadn't met before was with them. We hit it off immediately. Later we broke from the group. We walked and talked for hours. I forgot about the note and didn't open the note until the following morning. I knew that I met the love of my life. Before two weeks had passed, he proposed. Do you think that was the question?"

Epilog

Jonathan and Ashia honeymooned in Paris and visited the winery still run by Jean-Paul's family. They imagined that one of the small towns they toured was where Zack and Marie met again, years after the war. Jonathan and Ashia sat at a sidewalk café and pictured Marie and Zack, the 1922 lovers, walking hand in hand.

Several months after their wedding, Ashia and Jonathan received a wedding invitation.

Rebecca (Becky) Baron
and Reverend Joseph Meier
together with their parents
request the honor of your presence
at the celebration of their marriage
Saturday, the twenty-seventh of May
nineteen-hundred and ninety-two
at four p.m.

The service will be held at
Redemption Ridge Farm
RSVP

Zackarie Todd's story ran under Jonathan Dunquin's byline. Ed, Jonathan's old editor, paid well for it and complimented him with genuine appreciation. Jonathan finished ghost writing Ashia's father's memoirs.

Before his passing, Zack authorized his family to provide Jonathan with access to all the history of the farm, including the attic chest, and his and Marie's cards, notes, journals, and love letters. Marie kept every written message of love that she and Zack exchanged.

Ashia and Jonathan purchased a weekend retreat near the farm and visit often. They are copying all of Emmett and Hope's love letters as well as Sarah's many journals.

One day, Claire surprised Jonathan and Ashia with an old tin box that a carpenter found while repairing a portion of the gazebo floor. The content was well preserved, it contained declarations of love shared by the 1850 lovers, Rebecca and Joseph.

Jonathan and Ashia are co-authoring a book about the love that grew in the glow of reflected sunsets from Redemption Ridge. One of the stories will be about a love that lasted seventy-three years in the heart and mind of a wise friend. Others will tell of love that continues to grow over many lifetimes.

About the Author

George Eugene Belcher is retired from a career in advertising. He and Carole, his wife and soulmate of over half a century make their home in South Florida. *Return to Redemption Ridge* is his first published novel. His next novel will be released in late 2012.